THE RIGHTEOUS SMUGGLER

by DEBBIE SPRING

Second
Story
Press

Library and Archives Canada Cataloguing in Publication

Spring, Debbie, 1953-
The righteous smuggler / by Debbie Spring.

(The Holocaust remembrance series for young readers)
ISBN 1-896764-97-5
ISBN-13 978-1-896764-97-9

1. World War, 1939-1945--Children--Juvenile fiction.
2. World War, 1939-1945--Jews--Rescue--Juvenile fiction.
3. World War, 1939-1945--Netherlands--Amsterdam--Juvenile
fiction. I. Title. II. Series: Holocaust remembrance book for
young readers.

PS8587.P734R53 2005   jC813'.6   C2005-904222-2

Cover photo © Getty Images
Edited by Sarah Silberstein Swartz
Copyedited by Carolyn Jackson
Designed by P. Rutter

The views or opinions expressed in this book and the context in
which the images are used do not necessarily reflect the views or
policy of, nor imply approval or endorsement by, The United
States Holocaust Memorial Museum.

Printed and bound in Canada

*Second Story Press gratefully acknowledges the support of the Ontario
Arts Council and the Canada Council for the Arts for our publishing
program. We acknowledge the financial support of the Government of
Canada through the Book Publishing Industry Development Program.*

Published by
Second Story Press
20 Maud Street, Suite 401
Toronto, Ontario, Canada M5V 2M5

www.secondstorypress.ca

THE RIGHTEOUS SMUGGLER

For my devoted and dedicated husband, Fred. Thank you for all your feedback and support. And much appreciation to my family: Josh, Miriam and Oren.

Many thanks to: Margie Wolfe for her invaluable input and for believing in me; Sarah Schwartz for her wonderful editorial guidance; and the staff of Second Story Press for working hard to make this book a success.

PROLOGUE

THE GERMAN INVASION OF HOLLAND began on May 10, 1940. It was a complete surprise and shock to the Dutch people. Holland expected to remain neutral, as it had been during World War I. The occupation was swift. The Nazis introduced many changes and forced everyone to carry identity cards. Without them, the Dutch could not get ration coupons to buy food.

Persecution of Dutch Jews began as soon as the Nazi invaded. The letter 'J' was stamped on all the Dutch Jewish identity cards, allowing the Nazis to trace all the Jews of Holland. Evening curfews kept everyone off the street. During the bombings, the Dutch put up black curtains and sat in the dark to keep their homes from being targets. Many ran to underground shelters when the bombing started. Holland had a large Jewish population of about 140,000; 90,000 members of the Jewish community lived in its capital city, Amsterdam. Between May of 1940 and the summer of 1941, Jews gradually disappeared from public life. Jews were not allowed in hotels or restaurants. Their land was taken away and sold to non-Jews. By February of 1941 mass arrests of Jews had begun.

Jewish areas were raided and many Jews, both young and old, were beaten up and taken away to concentration camps, never to be seen again.

The war caused the deaths of 240,000 Dutch people, 106,000 of whom were Jews. During World War II, at least 250,000 Gypsies and six million Jews were systematically murdered in Europe. It was these acts of genocide against the Jews and Gypsies that were classified as crimes against humanity in trials held by the Allies after the war.

The response of the people in Holland toward the persecution of Jews was mixed. As many as 45,000 Dutch men and boys volunteered to assist the German occupiers. Some Dutch people did fight back. Anne Frank wrote this in her diary about the resistance movement in Holland:

"There are a great number of organizations, such as 'The Free Netherlands', which forge identity cards, supply money to people underground, find hiding places for people...it is amazing how much noble, unselfish work these people are doing (by) risking their own lives to help and save others."

The Righteous Smuggler is historical fiction about an ordinary, young gentile boy who made a difference by risking his life to save Jewish families, because he had learned that every life counted. Although the characters and sequence of events portrayed in this story are fictitious, the invasion, occupation, anti-Jewish measures, and resistance are true to history. There really were some people much like Hendrik and his family.

Just as we cannot forget the Holocaust, we must never forget those courageous individuals, the 'righteous gentiles,' who risked their own lives to save the lives of Jews. They proved that goodness, compassion, and selflessness did exist.

* * *

PART ONE

OCCUPATION
1940

CHAPTER 1
SOS

Proudly, I raised the Dutch flag on Papa's fishing boat. I was the luckiest guy in the world to be living in Amsterdam. I couldn't imagine living anywhere else. I loved everything about my city. I loved its familiar streets and its canals. I loved the fact that the docks were so close to the streets of the city and that our boat could float along the narrow canals. These canals branched throughout Amsterdam, connecting the city to the North Sea and Holland's lush countryside.

As we drifted along in our boat, floating under the bridges, I took in the familiar sights and sounds of the streets on both sides of the canal. Above us, cars, bicycles, and pedestrians travelled the red cobblestone roads. We passed a park that looked like a sea of vibrant red and yellow tulips as far as the eye could see. My mouth watered as we passed the many busy shops. I could smell the fresh-baked bread and watch the carts carrying the round yellow and orange Gouda cheeses as big as my head. As we passed the Jewish quarter, I saw my friend Malka entering her synagogue with her family.

After school and on weekends, I got to do this — my favorite thing — go fishing with my Papa. I breathed in the salty air. There was such a feeling of freedom when we were out in the boat. The wind blew my bangs into my eyes. The cool air made red circles on my cheeks. The boat rocked continuously back and forth, like Mama used to rock me gently in her arms.

Papa did not speak to me all afternoon. That was his way. But when he spoke, I listened. Mostly he talked without words. His body had a language of its own. When he pointed, I fetched. And when he curled his fingers upwards, that meant come here.

Papa broke off a chunk of bread and sliced some cheese, handing it to me.

I munched on the food and licked my dry lips.

"Happy birthday, Hendrik."

I blinked. "I thought you had forgotten."

"It's May 10, 1940 isn't it?" he teased.

"Of course, it is," I replied.

"You were born on May 10, 1928. That should make you how old today?"

"I'm twelve today."

"My goodness, Hendrik Vandinther, you are almost a man." Papa smiled. "What would you like for your birthday present?"

"A ball," I answered without hesitation, "so that I can play soccer with the guys."

"You don't mind a used ball, do you?" asked Papa, who was always concerned about money.

"As long as it doesn't have holes," I laughed.

Papa looked relieved. "I'll see what I can do."

I felt a strong tug as my fishing rod bent. "I've got a bite!" I yelled.

"Reel her in, nice and easy," said Papa.

But suddenly my father's attention was elsewhere. The wireless radio crackled: "May Day, May Day." Papa answered the call. "What's your location?"

Though I did not want to lose my fish, I was curious to know who was in trouble and had sent out the distress signal. Reeling in my line too quickly, I lost my fish. "Papa what is it?"

He put his finger to his lips, gesturing to me to be quiet. He wrote down some directions as he spoke. "Nobody has answered your distress call? I'm surprised. Don't worry, I'll be there in about one hour."

Papa signed off and pointed to a spot on his map. "That's where the distress signal is coming from. The people in trouble have been pulled out by the strong currents of the North Sea. They are drifting north toward Denmark."

"But Papa, that's at least an hour out to sea and it will be another two hours back. What about my birthday party? Mama said that I could have my friends over. My friends will be waiting."

"Hendrik, these people are in trouble. We must think of them first."

"Let someone else help them. It's not fair. I only have a party once a year." From his wrinkled brow, I could see that

Papa was losing patience with me.

"They need help and we are the closest boat to them."

Again my curiosity got the better of me. "Papa, what happened to them?"

"They are French tourists with no boating experience. They rented a fishing boat, went out for too long, and ran out of fuel. The strong current pulled them out to sea. Remember, Hendrik, we must always help when people are in trouble. What if you were in trouble and nobody would help you? Hmm?"

"Fine," I grumbled.

"Cheer up. I'm sure that your friends will wait for you."

We headed out to sea. Papa steered in the upper deck's cabin, while I sat on the wooden bench on the main deck. The waves became choppier and our boat, which was the size of a bus, bobbed up and down as we sped along with our motor churning up the water, making a V with its wake. "Keep a look out for a stalled boat," said Papa.

I shielded my eyes from the sun with my hand and stared into the horizon. What rotten luck. This unexpected adventure was spoiling my birthday. "Papa, why do you always have to be such a do-gooder? Why can't I come first for a change?" I knew that I was being bold, but sometimes I just blurted out what I thought instead of keeping it inside. I waited for Papa to tell me that I was being selfish.

He sighed and did not speak for a while. He seemed lost in thought.

Finally he spoke. "Hendrik, I have never told you the story of when I was a boy your age."

"You've told me many stories, Papa."

"It's the story about my younger brother."

I gasped. "You have a brother?"

Papa nodded. "I had a baby brother, Stefan." He took a deep breath and started telling the story.

"One day, I took out my father's boat with my brother. My father said that I was seaworthy enough to manage on my own and the weather conditions were calm. I felt very grown-up. But I was so busy showing off to my brother, acting like a rooster, that I forgot to watch the wind and current, and to listen to the weather report. I remembered to boss my brother around, but I forgot to take compass readings. I did a lot of stupid things.

"When the fog rolled in, I forgot to stay close to shore. We ate a big hearty lunch that our mother had made for us. But then I got sleepy. I left my brother in charge of the steering wheel, while I took a nap. When I woke up, I didn't know where we were. Because of the fog, I couldn't tell the land from the sea and I had no idea which way was north.

"The current and winds took us far out to sea. I used the ship radio and called for help, but I couldn't tell my father or other seamen my co-ordinates. What a fool I had been. I couldn't control the boat and eventually we capsized. Somehow I managed to lower the wooden rowboat into the water and I got myself and Stefan safely into it." Papa took a few deep breaths.

I was stunned. I thought I knew all of Papa's stories but I never knew that Papa had a younger brother. That meant I had an Uncle Stefan, which was news to me. "Go on, Papa."

"Stefan and I took turns rowing until our arms felt like lead. Then we drifted. Perhaps I wouldn't have been so angry if no one had seen us. But a cargo ship went right by us. When we screamed and waved, the captain beeped his horn at us. To my shock and horror, he didn't stop to help. He was probably in a hurry and thought that someone else would help us.

"Hours passed under the scorching sun and finally, to our relief, another boat came by and stopped. But they wouldn't take us aboard because they were crossing the Atlantic Ocean, not returning to Holland. They promised to send help and we believed them. We thought we were saved. As we waited and waited, our hopes faded. They never did send a rescue party. No boats came by after that.

"I decided then and there that if I lived through this experience, and if ever anyone was in trouble, I wouldn't wait for the next boat. I would be the one to help." After this long speech, Papa seemed to run out of steam. He just sat there in the stern with his head in his hands.

"What happened next? How were you saved?" I asked.

"We weren't saved." Papa replied and stopped short.

"Please, Papa. I need to know," I pleaded. "Please go on with your story."

* * *

CHAPTER 2
PAPA'S STORY

PAPA SIGHED AND CONTINUED. *"Stefan was a scrawny little guy. I was older and bigger. I always liked my mother's cooking and often took large helpings and seconds. You might say that I was on the chunky side and strong, while my brother was more delicate.*

"I don't know how many days we drifted in the hot sun without food and water. The cooler nights brought relief, but we both shivered from our sunburns. Stefan's chattering teeth kept me awake.

"Finally, I saw land and I decided we had to save ourselves. It was too rocky to land with the rowboat. I had to make a decision. If we stayed on the boat, we would keep drifting out to sea. We must risk it and swim for shore, even if it meant I had to tow my brother.

"Just as I was getting up my nerve to begin the long swim, we saw a dorsal fin. That could only mean one thing — a shark. We froze in fear. It circled us for most of the day. Sometimes it rammed itself underneath the boat, making a loud thunk. Once it nearly threw us out of the rowboat.

"Stefan begged me to do something. He was shaking with fright. I timed it, and when the shark, with its sharp teeth

showing, came close to my side, I took an oar and hit its body with all my might. The oar snapped in half. Now we had only one oar. My heart thumped as though I were running a marathon. But it worked, and the shark swam away for the moment. I knew that it would be back. A shark will wait until it wears out its prey, and then it strikes again. And this shark could easily destroy our boat with a few more whacks."

"Then what Papa?"

"When I told Stefan we would both have to swim for it before the shark returned, Stefan began to cry that he was too weak to make the swim himself. I tried to console him. It was then that I made my promise. I promised not to leave him and to save him — a promise that I couldn't keep."

Now Papa was overcome with his feelings. He took off his old blue cap, the one that Mama had knitted for him, and wiped his hand through his hair.

I took Papa's hand and squeezed it. "It's okay, Papa."

Papa closed his eyes as he relived the past. *"I draped one arm across Stefan and towed him along with me, as I swam in the frigid sea. The cold took my breath away. I swallowed salty water that burned my parched throat. The waves thrashed against me until I was exhausted, but I wouldn't let go of my brother. We banged up against the rocks and my leg began to bleed. I prayed that the shark wouldn't be close enough to smell the blood. Sharks go into a feeding frenzy when they smell blood."*

"Did you make it to shore, Papa?"

"Yes, we did."

"Then how did you break your promise? And where is Stefan now?" I asked.

Papa looked at the sky as the tears welled in his eyes. "Stefan...." Papa wiped his tears. I had never seen him cry before. "He's in heaven." Papa slumped for a moment, and then continued.

"When we came to shore, Stefan couldn't stop shaking and coughing. I don't know if he died from exposure, pneumonia, starvation, or thirst. I only know that I held him in my arms until my father and a search party found us. Even though Stefan felt bone cold and I couldn't feel a pulse, I still held him close to me."

We were both silent for a long time. It had taken a lot out of Papa to tell his story. Papa may have made foolish mistakes, but he didn't deserve to lose his brother. He blamed himself for not saving him. Why hadn't anyone helped them?

Then my mind returned to the present and I remembered how I had tried to talk Papa out of helping this couple. "Let someone else save them," I had said. Now I felt ashamed.

Across the horizon, I saw a small dot. "There they are." I pointed to the right. "Off to the starboard side."

* * *

CHAPTER 3
SAVED

As we got closer to the weathered, shabby-looking fishing boat, I saw a man and a woman huddled together, shivering on the deck. They looked very scared and cold. "Bonjour!" the man shouted. They were dressed in short-sleeved tops with no jackets, not proper attire for the sea. Experience boaters know that even though the sun may be bright, the wind at sea is strong and cold. When they came aboard our boat, they did a lot of talking, but it was all in French. Though I didn't understand a word, Papa had a little French. He tied their boat to ours.

"*Froid,*" said the woman, shivering.

I understood that meant that she was cold, so I ran down the stairs and got two wool blankets. She kissed me on both cheeks and I blushed. Papa served them hot tea from his thermos. They looked very grateful.

Now I understood what Papa had meant. What would have become of them if we hadn't gone to help them? I thought about what I had said to Papa, about letting someone else rescue them because I wanted my birthday party. Their gratitude made me feel ashamed again and I hung my head.

The woman stuck out her lip and shrugged. I thought that she wanted me to explain why I was sad. "Papa, how do you say birthday in French?"

"Bonne fête," he said, pointing at me.

The woman nodded that she understood and elbowed her husband, whereupon he took out his wallet. Papa shook his head 'no'. Instead, the nice lady reached into her bag and handed me a chocolate. I looked at Papa to see if this was okay. He smiled. Before Papa could change his mind, I popped the dark chocolate into my mouth and let it melt. That way it would last longer. I smiled at the wonderful flavor. All three of them began to laugh.

"What's so funny?" I asked Papa.

"You have chocolate all over your mouth."

When we got back, it was dark. It was too late to sell our fish. Papa would not make any money this day. I could say goodbye to my soccer ball. We docked in our usual spot, opposite the marine shop where Papa bought his nets and hooks. I jumped on the wooden wharf and quickly tied our boat to the dock, using three half hitches. I was good at doing fishermen knots, so this was always my job. After warm handshakes all around, Papa and I said goodbye to the French couple.

The streets were now almost empty with few cars and bicycles out at this time of night. The man with the apple cart had long gone home, along with the other merchants who sold their wares on the street.

When we got home, the yellow and red tulips in our front garden and on the windowsill gave me a warm feeling. I wiped my clogs on the welcome mat and prayed that my friends were waiting for me. My heart sank like an anchor. The house was empty except for Mama doing needlepoint in her rocking chair by the fireplace. She was already in her nightgown. She started to scold. But when Papa put up his hand, she stopped. He told Mama the story of the French couple out at sea and how, if it hadn't been for us, they could have drowned or died of thirst or cold.

Mama nodded in approval. "It is important to help those in need," she agreed. We sat at the oak table while Mama served us the dinner she had saved. It had gone stone cold, but I knew enough not to complain. I was so hungry that I didn't mind and I shovelled in the cold soup. For dessert, Mama had baked an apple strudel especially for my birthday. It was mouth-watering. I hugged her. "Mama, you're the best baker in the whole wide world."

"Thank you, Hendrik. Now get ready for bed."

As I lay in bed with my feather comforter, I remembered the taste of the chocolate. I was sad that I had missed my own birthday party, but I was glad that we had saved the French couple. I couldn't wait to tell the story to my friends tomorrow.

Later that night, I was startled by the sound of the shrill police sirens. There was shouting in the streets. I ran downstairs and peeked through the flowered curtains.

"Go back to bed, Hendrik," said Mama.

"What's happening?" I asked.

"I don't know." Mama turned on the radio.

The radio announced: "The Germans have invaded Holland."

Mama gasped. "No, this can't be happening."

Papa paced the room like a tiger in a small cage. Mama prayed.

"I don't understand," I said.

Papa sat me down beside him. "It's like when you were tiny and played in the sandbox. Another little boy had a toy truck and you wanted it, so you just took it. Of course, I made you give it back."

"But I didn't know any better," I said.

"People and governments get greedy, Hendrik. Hitler, the leader of Germany, is greedy. He wants to conquer and take other countries, including the Netherlands."

"But can't we teach him to not be greedy?" I asked.

"I wish it were that easy," said Papa.

"Now get to bed, Hendrik," insisted Mama. She shooed me off, wiping her tears. Papa hugged me and then her.

Because I didn't want my birthday to be over, I tried to stay awake. But the sounds of fighting in the streets — gunshots and police sirens — made me hide under the covers. With the pillow over my head, I tried to drown out the noises of the night. Deep down inside, I knew that I would never forget this birthday, May 10, 1940. I didn't know what would happen now that the Germans had invaded my country, but I had a sinking feeling that this might be the birthday when everything I knew and loved changed forever.

CHAPTER 4
TANKS IN THE STREETS

FOR THE NEXT COUPLE OF DAYS, I was not allowed to leave the house. This made me stir crazy. I was used to running outside all day, and staying in made me feel as though I were sick. I wondered what my friends were doing. Were they kept inside their homes as well? My parents listened to all the news reports on the radio. It could not be good news because Mama kept wringing her hands and Papa kept pacing across the room.

"I'm going out to see what is going on," Papa announced. Mama pleaded with him to stay inside. "Don't worry, I'll be careful," he said as he prepared to leave.

"Can I go, too?" I asked. I wanted to see the fighting for myself. "Can I, Papa?"

"No." Papa looked stern.

"But Papa, I don't want to miss all of the excitement."

He took me by the shoulders. "This is not a game, Hendrik." He called to my mother, "I'll be back soon, dear."

While Papa was gone, Mama jumped at every sound. I had never seen her so nervous. She kept peeking out the curtains to see what was happening in the street. But she

would not let me even go near the window. I tried to do my homework but I couldn't concentrate. When would Papa be home? I wanted to know what was happening.

When Papa walked through the front door, Mama threw her arms around him. He stroked her hair and comforted her.

"Tell me, Papa, what's happening in the streets?" I blurted out.

He collapsed on the sofa and I ran to get him his slippers. He smiled gratefully and changed out of his clogs. "It's over. In just these last few days, the Germans have seized all the important areas of Holland. Our prime minister and his cabinet have left for England, where they have set up a government in exile." Papa hung his head. "I'm afraid that Holland was forced to surrender. Now the Nazis rule over us. Mark my words, Hendrik, there will be many changes and they won't be good."

For a short while, there was an eerie quiet in the streets. Then everything changed again as people rushed out into the street. Without permission, I ran outside, banging the wooden door behind me.

At first I thought that there was a parade because so many people jammed the streets. I wove my way in and out of the crowd to the front. Army tanks with the German flag crawled down the center of the road. German soldiers marched in straight rows stomping in rhythm in their tall black boots. They raised one arm in front of them and cried out in unison, "*Heil Hitler!*"

I fought my way through the crowds and found my best friend, Pieter. Pieter's parents owned the fish store where Papa sold his catch. When we saw each other, we were so excited that we both tried to talk at the same time.

"All the shops are closed," said Pieter.

I looked around. "All the Dutch flags are gone from the shops and homes, and that ugly swastika has taken their places. It looks like a horrible spider."

"My parents told me that the Germans would never attack Holland and now they have." Pieter shuddered.

He handed me a lemon drop and I sucked on it, enjoying the sour taste. But another sour taste rose in my throat when I saw Eric. He was the class bully and liked to pick on me and Pieter. 'I'm not afraid, I'm not afraid,' I repeated in my head, trying to convince myself. So what if he is so much taller than me? So what if he's the size of an ox? I tried to will him away, but — my bad luck — he made a beeline toward us. He walked right up to Pieter and shoved him. Pieter went flying. But the streets were so crowded that he was bumped into a stout man and didn't hurt himself.

"Watch where you are going," the man scolded. Pieter mumbled an apology.

Eric came after Pieter again. "Dirty Jew!" he yelled.

I was boiling inside. How could he call my best friend names? I punched at Eric, but only hit the air as he ducked out of the way.

Eric grabbed my arm and twisted it behind my back.

"Fool, I'm not after you. I'm after the Jew." He spit on the ground. "You better find yourself another playmate soon or next time I'll be after your hide." Eric let go and my arm throbbed. I rubbed my shoulder. There was a fight going on down the street. Fortunately, this interested Eric and he took off to join in. I felt weak and ashamed.

"What's wrong, Hendrik?" asked Pieter.

"I wish I had belted Eric right in the mouth and taught him a lesson, once and for all."

"It's not your fault, said Pieter. "You can't fight someone bigger and stronger than you."

"But you can sure try," I replied.

* * *

CHAPTER 5
TAKING A STAND

AS WE GOT CLOSER TO THE FIGHTING DOWN THE STREET, I could see what was happening. A gang of boys had circled a pregnant woman.

"We don't need any more Jews being born," cried a boy who looked no older than me.

Eric joined in, knocking the woman's hat off. Someone else pushed her down. They surrounded her, shouting and swearing. She curled up, protecting her belly. Was I as bad as those bullies? I wasn't the one hurting the woman, but I was allowing her to be hurt by not stopping them. Those boys were acting like wild animals. They could harm the woman and her unborn baby. But I was outnumbered.

Pieter pulled at my sleeve. "There's nothing we can do. Let's get out of here."

Suddenly I had an idea.

"Where are you going?" asked Pieter as I started running toward a garbage can. Thankfully, there were newspapers in it. I searched in my pocket for matches. I often carried matches and a pocketknife, because they came in handy on the boat for fixing frayed rope. My heart pounded as I lit the newspaper in the garbage can. As it went up in flames, I shouted, "Fire! Run!"

Eric and the other bullies saw the flames rising behind them and ran off in different directions. Pieter and I hurried over to the pregnant woman on the ground and helped her up. Her legs were scraped and bleeding. The two of us helped her walk away.

"My baby," she cried. "Please let it be okay." Her face was pale.

"Your baby will be fine," I panted, trying to catch my breath.

"Where are you taking me?" Panic rose in her voice.

"Somewhere safe," I said, squeezing her hand to reassure her.

We took her to Malka's father's bakery. Mr. Mendel was kind and I knew he would help her.

Malka was minding the store. Luckily, it was empty. "What's happened?" she asked as we rushed in.

"Get your parents. This woman is hurt and has been badly scared," I said.

Malka raced upstairs where she lived and came down with her parents.

"Oh, dear," said Mr. Mendel, when he saw the bleeding woman.

Mrs. Mendel ran back upstairs and returned with a bowl of water and bandages. She cleaned the woman's wounds. The woman was crying and holding her belly. Mrs. Mendel talked quietly to her.

Pieter explained what had happened, how I had lit a fire to scare the bullies away.

Malka looked at me with a strange look. Was she proud of me? I blushed from head to toe.

"Thank you kindly, boys," said the woman.

"You're welcome." Suddenly I felt very tired. "If you don't need me, I'm going home."

"Wait," said Mr. Mendel. He handed me a loaf of pumpernickel bread. He knew that it was my favorite because I always bought it.

"I don't have any money," I said.

"It's a gift," said Mr. Mendel. "For helping."

"No, I couldn't," I said. But he was insistent, so I took the bread. As I headed out, the pregnant woman was buying two loaves of egg bread. It was her way of repaying the Mendels for taking her in.

Pieter followed me outside. "Can I come over?" he asked.

Tired, I nodded yes. Like my father, I sometimes talked without words. Pieter understood me and we walked home together without a further word. It was a comfortable silence. I felt as though a big weight had been lifted from my shoulders. I giggled.

"What's so funny?" asked Pieter.

"I took on an entire gang. And to think that just a few minutes before, I was afraid of Eric."

Pieter smiled and slapped me on the back. Soon we were both howling with laughter.

When we came to my place, Papa welcomed us with open arms. "In the excitement of these last days, Hendrik, I forgot to give you your birthday present." Papa opened the closet and took out a soccer ball.

"Thanks, Papa!" I grabbed the ball and examined it. The words 'School Property' were printed across the white ball. Papa's face reddened in embarrassment. "I bought it from the school for a good price." He grabbed his pen and crossed out the words and wrote my name on the ball. The smell of fresh ink filled the air. Sure I would have preferred a new ball, but at least it was all mine and I could play with it outside of school hours.

"I love it," I said, smiling at him. Papa's face brightened up. "Come on, Pieter, let's play soccer in the park," I suggested.

When we got to the park there was a new sign. "Probably says, stay off the grass," I said. "As if I would pay attention to that."

Pieter's face turned white as he read the sign.

"What does it say?" I moved closer and read the sign by the park bench.

'No dogs or Jews allowed.'

I was outraged. Pieter and I always played in this park and nobody was going to tell me otherwise. "Come on." I kicked the ball to Pieter. He looked around nervously, as if a policeman was going to give him a ticket, and he missed the ball.

"Pay attention, Pieter!" I yelled. Then he ran after the ball and kicked it back.

Soon we were running everywhere, getting mud all over ourselves. It was just like old times. I desperately needed to feel normal and this was doing the trick. Pieter was my best friend. We felt like brothers — and brothers took care of each other.

* * *

CHAPTER 6
THE CINEMA

"I HAVE A SURPRISE FOR YOU," said Pieter.

"You do?" I asked. My eyes lit up.

"Two tickets to the cinema."

"Thank you so much, Pieter." I didn't even care what was playing. I never had enough money to go to the cinema. Now I could hardly contain my excitement.

"What are you waiting for?" smiled Pieter. "Race you!" And off we went. I was faster, but this time I let Pieter win. After all, he was treating.

We entered the cinema. It smelled of fresh popcorn and my mouth watered. Pieter bought popcorn and shared it with me. We sat down in our seats and waited for the magic to begin.

A news clip came on first. It was in German, and I knew only a few words of German. Hitler's face, with its straight black moustache, filled the screen. Soldiers saluted him and yelled out his name. I slouched in my seat. This wasn't fair. I came in here to get away from the real world, but it had followed me inside. I was grateful when the main feature finally started.

Soon, I was captivated by the film and I forgot my troubles. I loved the way the cowboy chased after the bad guy on horseback. I was swept away by the adventures of the hero escaping on horseback from a mob, rescuing the beautiful maiden. The cowboy made it look so easy. One man took on an entire army. I wanted to be just like him.

When we left the dark theater, I blinked in the sunlight, like a mole. Pieter made fun of me. We laughed and talked about cowboys and the Wild West.

We saw the theater owner putting up a new sign. "Maybe he's advertising which picture will be playing next. Let's go see," I said.

The sign said 'No Jews allowed.' I felt angry. Pieter bit his lip. We both walked away. "Has Hitler brainwashed everybody?" I asked. "Has everyone lost their minds?"

Pieter shoved his hands into his pockets and walked fast. I hurried to keep up. "You'll see, they'll lose a lot of business if Jews aren't allowed in. Then they'll be sorry," I said.

As we walked, Pieter became happier again. His eyes twinkled. "I still have a little money left. We could buy an ice cream to share."

I was already salivating. "Yes, let's." I led the way.

We stopped in our tracks when we reached the ice cream parlor. I hesitated before I spoke. "There's that horrible sign again. If you want, I'll go in and order the ice cream and bring it out for you," I said apologetically.

"No. I'm not hungry any more." Pieter headed for home. "See you tomorrow." He waved goodbye.

"Thanks for the film," I called after him.

CHAPTER 7
BLACKOUT

"THIS SOUP TASTES LIKE WATER," I complained at dinner. Mama left the room, hurt by my comments. Papa glared at me.

"What did I say wrong?" But I knew exactly what I was doing. I was so frustrated that I was looking for a fight.

"Your mother is trying her best, under the circumstances," said Papa, wrinkling his forehead. "Since the Germans have invaded Holland, it's hard to get staples like meat, flour, or sugar. And we're the lucky ones. Some families don't even have fish to put in their soup. You should be ashamed of yourself."

Of course, I knew about the food rationing. The neighborhood grocery's shelves were almost empty. Now I felt like a slug and I wanted to hide under a rock. "I didn't mean to hurt Mama's feelings."

"Go and apologize."

"Yes, Papa."

By the time I got up the courage to apologize, Mama was busy putting up black curtains. "I'm sorry. You're the best cook in the world." Mama hugged me. That meant that I was forgiven. "What are you doing?" I asked.

31

"We have to darken our house, so that the light from inside our house doesn't attract attention. Any light could make our house a target for the bombs."

Bombing blackouts were exciting in war movies, but thinking that our house might be bombed was frightening. I helped Mama put up the heavy black fabric across the windows.

The Nazis now enforced curfews in the evenings for everyone in Amsterdam. No one was allowed in the streets after eight o'clock at night. I hated not being able to play outside after dinner. I hated not being able to spend an evening with Pieter or Jacob. I knew family was important, but too much family time got on my nerves. Mama never sat still and kept finding new projects. They always entailed cleaning or organizing — and they always included me. She even made me sweep the attic. I kept hoping that she would run out of chores.

Later that night, I had my first taste of a real blackout. It seemed so strange in the early evening to sit in the dark after the sirens went off. I couldn't even read by candlelight, since any light could make us a target for the planes flying overhead. Even though the airplanes flying over us might be our friends, the Allies, we were still in great danger of being bombed by them.

I stuffed cotton balls in my ears to drown out the blaring sirens. I never got used to these blackouts, even though they seemed to happen every night. I longed for the quiet, peaceful hours when Mama played Chopin on the piano and Papa hammered in his workshop.

During the days, I went to school, as usual, but in the evenings I couldn't bear spending another hour trapped inside. On occasion, I went over to my neighbor Johan's after school. His mother was gentile, but his father was a non-practising Jew. Johan had been baptized and went to the same church as we did. That's why he didn't live in the Jewish district. Mama thought that he was a little too wild for me, but I reassured her that he wasn't. I had a good time at his house, playing poker. We placed bets with stones rather than with money. I was down five stones, but I didn't care because it beat the long monotonous evenings at home. When the blackout happened, I was happy that I was there safely inside.

Johan whispered into my ear. "Let's sneak outside for a smoke."

I was shocked. "I don't..."

"Shhh," he whispered. "My parents are in bed."

It had been a while since I had done anything rebellious. "Okay," I said.

* * *

CHAPTER 8
THE PROMISE

WE STOOD BY THE BACK OF HIS HOUSE AND LIT UP. "Since when do you smoke?" I asked.

He shrugged. "My father smokes, so why shouldn't I?"

"Won't he be angry if he finds out?"

"So what? He always told me to act like a man, so I am."

Who could argue with that logic? I inhaled and had a coughing fit. Johan laughed and blew smoke rings.

I wished that I could do that, too. When I tried, I doubled up from coughing.

All of a sudden, Johan's cigarette was pulled from his mouth.

Johan's father stood in his housecoat and he looked as angry as a hornet. "Johan, are you crazy?"

I quickly stomped out my cigarette.

"But you smoke, Father."

"That's the least of my worries, you silly boy. You could get killed over a stupid cigarette. If the bombers flying overhead see even a flicker of light, kaboom, you're a target."

Johan's face turned ashen. "It won't happen again, Father," he said in a small voice.

"It better not. Boys, come inside."

"It's getting late. I'd better go home," I said.

"It's dangerous out there," said Johan's father. "You'll sleep here tonight."

"But I live so close by," I said.

"Any step outside is dangerous during an air raid. You'll sleep over and that's an order."

"Yes, sir. I'll ring my parents and let them know."

We went back inside. I was glad that he had ordered me to stay. There was a loud crash and then a fire truck went by. My house was just a few doors down the street, but it seemed very far away at the moment. My parents agreed that I should stay at Johan's house overnight. When Johan's father had gone back to bed, I lay down on a cot in Johan's room. We talked about girls and soccer. I already felt better.

"I have a crush on Esther," said Johan.

"Esther will never be allowed to go out with you because her parents only allow her to date Jewish boys," I replied.

"Maybe I can convince her parents because I'm half-Jewish. For the first time, being Jewish could be to my advantage," he joked.

"Maybe," I said.

"It's crazy. I never practised being Jewish. I've always considered myself a Christian. I celebrate Christmas and go to mass, but all of a sudden the Nazis make us carry identity cards and mine says that I'm Jewish." Johan punched his pillow. "My mother was furious and called the authorities and got the priest to tell them that I'm baptized and Christian, but the German government doesn't see it that way. They said that they now go back generations to check to see if there are any Jews in the family. If you ask me, if you go back far enough, we're all Jewish. After all, Jesus was Jewish." Johan's face was red. "It doesn't make any sense. The whole world has gone crazy."

"It's stupid," I agreed.

"It's more than stupid, it's dangerous. I'm trying to convince my parents that we have to leave Holland before it's too late."

"Before it's too late?" I asked.

"Before Hitler kills all the Dutch Jews and, apparently, now I'm one of them." Johan paced, picking up things and putting them down again.

For once, I didn't know what to say.

"Geography works against me."

"What do you mean?" I gulped.

"Holland is flat with no place to run and few places to hide. The countries bordering the Netherlands are all German-occupied. Flight across the Dutch border means going into another country controlled by Nazis. The west and north borders of the Netherlands are the North Sea coastline, where safe passage is almost impossible. The Germans patrol those waters so heavily that it is highly dangerous to travel near the coast." He stopped speaking and looked me straight in the face. "Would you hide me, if you had to?"

"Of course," I said without hesitation. "But it will never come to that. This war will last only a little longer and then everything will go back to normal. You'll see."

"Don't be so naive, Hendrik. Hitler is power hungry. Things will get worse. Think again about hiding me. If you were caught, you and maybe all of your family would be arrested and sent to a concentration camp. That's the new law."

"What's a concentration camp?" I asked.

"The Nazis say it's a work camp, but I've heard that nobody returns from these camps."

I shuddered. It was one thing to say that I would help someone and another to actually do it. Was it worth risking my life? But my father had taught me to help others. How could I not do what was right? I swallowed. "Yes, I would hide you and your family, Johan."

Johan came over and shook my hand. "Promise?"

"I promise."

"I hope that it doesn't come down to that. I hope that we will escape first."

"But if it does," I gulped, "I'll be there for you, I promise."

I didn't sleep well that night. Had I lost my mind? I had just made a promise to risk my life. My father had made the same kind of promise to his brother Stefan and couldn't keep it. Would I be able to keep my promise?

* * *

PART TWO

OPPRESSION
1941-1942

CHAPTER 9

ANTHEM

IT WAS GREAT TO GO BACK TO SCHOOL after the summer break. I was surprised because I normally loved my carefree summers. But this summer had been different. War had invaded every part of our lives. Soldiers with dogs and guns patrolled the streets. Guards continually stopped people to check their identity papers. It was dangerous not to carry your papers. There was a heavy fine if you couldn't produce them and if the guards were in a bad mood, they even arrested people.

Mama was overprotective and wouldn't let me ride my bike through the city any more. She wanted me to stay close to home. Money was tight. Fewer people could afford to buy Papa's fish from Pieter's parents' store. And then there were some clients who wouldn't buy anything from a Jew even if they had the money. Mama took in extra sewing to make ends meet. Because Mama was so busy, I had to run many of her errands.

I hoped school would mean a new start. This week had been filled with great excitement, catching up with friends, getting new books and new clothes, or at least slightly used 'new' ones.

Johan and I raced to school together. "I beat you!" I shouted.

"I'll win next time, Hendrik." Johan shared his last piece of milk chocolate with me, as we hurried to our seats.

"Where's Mr. Dusseldorf?" asked Johan. Whispers filled the class.

A new teacher in a Nazi uniform stood before us. "Mr. Dusseldorf is no longer with us. Stand for the German anthem," he ordered.

I remained sitting and so did some of my friends. Like my parents, I was proud to be Dutch. I had sung the Dutch national anthem my entire life. How dare the Germans tell us that we can no longer sing our own anthem?

The teacher's knuckles turned white as he gripped his ruler. "Those who don't stand will be punished — not by the principal, but by the police."

Now we were all scared. Johan, Pieter, Malka, Jacob, and I rose. I signalled to them by moving my finger across my lips. They nodded back at me and we all mimed zippering our lips closed. The teacher had forced us to stand, but we outsmarted him by only mouthing the words.

After the anthem, we sat down. What else would change, now that we had a German instead of a Dutch teacher? We all waited silently.

The new teacher tapped his ruler in his hand. "Take out your Dutch history books and give them to me." He walked around with a box, collecting our books. Reluctantly, I threw in mine. "You will learn only in German now," he declared.

My stomach cramped and I needed to go to the bathroom, but I dared not move. This new teacher was frightening.

"All Jewish children go home and don't come back," ordered the teacher.

Fear filled the room. Shocked, Pieter, Malka, and Jacob slowly rose and filed out the door. I stood to go with my friends to show support. I noticed that my friends, Hans and Josef, who went to my church, remained seated and silent. They wouldn't even make look me in the eye. Were they afraid?

The teacher looked at his list. "You are Hendrik Vandinther, correct?" he asked staring at me. "Sit down. You are not Jewish."

Reluctantly, I sat down.

The teacher studied the list again. Johan stared down at his knuckles. "Johan, you are Jewish. Leave now."

Johan turned beet red and knocked over his desk as he got up to leave.

"Pick it up," the teacher ordered. Johan picked up his desk and stormed out of the room.

It was hard for me to sit still. I felt like punching something. Johan, Pieter, Malka, and Jacob had been my friends since first grade. I never even thought of them as Jewish. They didn't think of me as Christian. We didn't care about religion. We only thought about ourselves as friends.

I stared at the empty seats and my heart felt empty, too.

"Turn to chapter four of your math textbooks."

We did our math, but I couldn't get any of the sums right. My mind was a million miles away. What would my friends do? Where would they go? What would I do without them? So many questions and no answers.

The teacher pointed to the equations on the board. "Hendrik? Do you know the answers to these questions?"

"No, sir." I wished I did!

The morning dragged on and became unbearable. My head was so full of tension it was like a pot ready to boil over. Recess, my favorite time, was even worse because my friends were gone. The yard, usually alive with laughing and chattering, was unusually quiet. Most of us were still in shock. Not Eric, of course. He was busy spitting out bad words about the Jews. I was so tired. All the strength had been sapped out of me. My friends had been banished and for what reason? I just wanted to go home and pretend this day had never happened.

* * *

CHAPTER 10
BLOOD BROTHERS

I SNUCK AWAY FROM THE SCHOOLYARD AND RAN HOME. It had started to rain, and now it began to pour. The high winds blew off my cap and I chased after it. I was not surprised to see Papa home. Last night, there had been a storm warning and Mama never allowed Papa to go out fishing in bad weather.

Mama wasn't home. Today was market day when the fresh cheese was sold, so Mama had gone out shopping. My mouth watered as I thought of the large round fresh Gouda and Havarti cheeses. "Papa, Papa!" I yelled, when I saw his boots at the front door.

"I'm in the workshop," he called.

I ran downstairs to the workshop where Papa mended his torn nets.

"What are you doing home?"

"Lunch time is earlier today," I lied. "I forgot my lunch so I came home."

I didn't know if Papa believed the story or not, but I needed to talk to him. Maybe he had some answers. "The Jews aren't allowed to go to school anymore and the new teacher says they're bad," I blurted out. "Pieter Goodman's Jewish and he's not bad." Papa listened, nodding his head in understanding. Although Papa was a man of few words, he was a good listener and he cared.

I finished up my lunch of sardines and buttermilk, and headed out the door, worrying about my best friend, Pieter. He had seemed pretty upset when he was ordered to leave. He probably needed me. Instead of going back to school, I headed toward Pieter's house.

It was only a ten-minute walk. The old Jewish quarter of Amsterdam was one of the poorest districts of the city, filled with alleys and slums. It housed many Jews from Eastern Europe, sometimes ten people in a one-family home. The streets were lined with Jewish shops and street vendors selling all kinds of goods. I passed the kosher butchers and the grocery store with wooden buckets filled with dill pickles. The area also attracted many writers and artists. One artist offered to do my portrait, but I showed him my empty pockets. I passed the old Portuguese Synagogue, which was the largest synagogue in the world. The surrounding building even had a library. I stopped to read the writing across the main entrance, but it was in Hebrew.

It was weird seeing so many children playing outside on a school day. But today was no ordinary day. Today was the day the Germans had taken over the schools.

German soldiers were everywhere. They wore swastika armbands and held guns. I was almost at Pieter's house when a soldier called out, "Dirty Jew." He spit at me and walked away. My body started to shake uncontrollably. I almost yelled after him, "Hey, you made a mistake, I'm not Jewish." But I kept my mouth shut. Was this what happened to Pieter whenever he walked in the streets? I shuddered.

As I came up to the front door of the Goodman's house I noticed a wooden box the size of my pointing finger on the left side of the doorframe. Mrs. Goodman let me in. "What's that for?" I asked pointing to the box.

She smiled. "That's called a mezuzah. Jewish people believe that it protects the house."

I entered and looked at the paintings that hung on the walls of their apartment. "I like your pictures. That one is my favorite." I pointed to a picture of the canals in Amsterdam.

"My brother painted it," said Mrs. Goodman, proudly. She went back to feeding the baby in his high chair. The baby's hands were in the bowl mashing the oatmeal. It was all over his face, hair, and clothes. It smelled as though he were ready for a diaper change. I wrinkled my nose.

"Pieter's upstairs in his room, but he won't come out. Please go talk to him." Mrs. Goodman took the baby out to change his diaper.

When I walked into Pieter's room, I was surprised to see his eyes red and swollen from crying. I had never seen Pieter cry before. Even when he fell from the tree and dislocated his shoulder and the doctor had to pop it back into place, Pieter didn't cry.

He blew his nose and made a honking sound. "I have a cold."

Pieter was embarrassed that I had caught him crying, so I pretended along with him. "I hope that I don't catch your cold." I took a big breath. "School is no fun without you there."

"Hendrik, you'd better go back to school or you'll get into trouble."

"I'm not going back. In science class, the German teacher erased Albert Einstein's name from the board. He says that Einstein is Jewish, so we no longer will be studying him."

"That's terrible," said Pieter. "But at least you can still go to school. It's worse being stuck at home. I love my parents, but they are so full of fear that they won't let me play outside. It's boring at home."

"I hate school," I sulked.

"Hendrik, you'd better go back. You're going to get into a lot of trouble."

"I don't care."

"At least go back for me and tell me what I'm missing," said Pieter.

"I promise I'll go back tomorrow."

"Soon you'll forget about me and you'll get a new best friend," mumbled Pieter.

"Never. You'll always be my best friend," I said. And then a great idea popped into my head. "Pieter, let's become blood brothers."

Pieter's eyes brightened.

We both pricked our fingers with a pin and, when they

bled, held them together. "That means that our blood joins us and nothing can change that. We are bonded. Friends, forever," I said.

"Friends, forever," repeated Pieter.

We both belted out the Dutch anthem. It made us feel proud and free.

"I've got to go," I said. "If I don't get home at my regular time, Mama will find out that I skipped class." Pieter walked me to the front door. "I'll visit tomorrow after school. Unless I have a detention for skipping today," I added.

My feeling of happiness evaporated as soon as I hit the streets. I saw a group of soldiers yelling at a religious Jew. Religious Jews were easy targets, I guess, because they looked different. They dressed in black hats and black coats and had long sideburns. Thank goodness the soldiers didn't hurt him. They only took his prayer book and stomped on it. After they left, the man picked up his book and kissed it.

On the way home, I came across Papa in front of our church, tearing down the German flag that the soldiers had hung there. I was proud of him, but scared for him at the same time.

* * *

CHAPTER 11
OBEDIENCE

THE NEXT DAY, WHEN I ARRIVED AT SCHOOL, I expected a detention. But so much had gone on that no one seemed to have noticed my absence. The seating plan was different. Everyone had moved to fill in the empty seats of their Jewish classmates and the extra desks had been taken away. It was as if they had never existed. I shuddered. I thought of a barrel of water. If you took out a cup of water, the water for a moment was disturbed, but then it went back to looking normal. If you looked hard enough, the level was slightly lower, but who looked hard enough? It was a scary thought that people were missing, but were not missed. Many of the other kids tried to act as though everything was the same as before. Were they blind?

We now had to speak only in German. Dutch was no longer allowed. The teacher handed out our German grammar textbooks. I opened the book up and froze. My friend Jacob's name was in the book. This was his textbook. His nose was always in a book. The teacher's voice droned on, but my head was in another space. Didn't anyone else but me see that this was all wrong? Jacob had been the smartest boy in the class.

Why wasn't he allowed to be here while Eric, who often failed his tests, was still allowed in class?

I tuned in when the teacher pulled out a cartoon drawing of a religious Jew. The teacher's teeth were stained brown from smoking and so were his fingers. "You can recognize Jews by their large beaks," he announced. I stared at the picture. The nose looked like a bent hawk's beak with troll-like hairs coming from its nostrils. "They wear beards to hide their ugly faces and long black coats to hide the things they steal."

What was he talking about? Why was he making up such lies? My face was burning.

"Why does the Jew wear a big black hat?" the teacher asked.

"Because he's hiding something?" asked Hans.

"Correct," said the teacher, smiling. "He's hiding the horns under his hat. Jews are the devil."

I felt like retching. How could Hans believe this nonsense? The teacher continued with ridiculous stories about how Jews took all of our money. Malka's father was a baker and he gave free bread to the poor. Jacob's father owned a bookstore and Jacob wore only hand-me-down clothes. Pieter's father bought and sold our fish in his market store. None of them were rich and none of them stole money from anyone else.

I looked around the classroom. Some of my classmates were busy taking notes. What was wrong with Hans, Ger, and Josef? They weren't Jew-haters, but they were going along with everything. Were they just too scared to speak out? Like sheep following the leader, they were obedient. Yet they had been brought up to be devout Christians and to do unto others as they would do unto you.

At recess, I tried to talk some sense into my friends. "Hans, how can you believe that all Jews lie and cheat? Did Pieter ever cheat you?"

"No."

"See?" I said.

"But when he grows up he will," said Hans.

I was shocked that nice people like Hans could be so easily swayed. How could he think this? He used to play soccer with Pieter.

"Hendrik is a Jew-lover," piped in Eric. "Jew-lover, Jew-lover!" he taunted.

This was not going the way that I had hoped. It was strange, but I was no longer afraid of Eric. After all, I had outsmarted him and the other hoodlums by saving the pregnant woman. Now I stared him down. "Get out of my way," I said as I pushed by him.

Eric looked surprised, but he was not entirely convinced that I had become a new person. He followed me and challenged me again. "Jew-lover!"

I pointed up behind him. "Look over there." Eric turned to look. "Made you look," I teased boldly. The other boys laughed at Eric. His face turned red. The school bell saved me. We filed back inside.

The only way that I could sit in class for the rest of the day was to dream that I was out fishing with Papa. I drew a picture of myself catching a fish. The sea wind was in my face. My fishing rod was bent right over as I pulled in the biggest fish ever. Papa had the net ready. I could smell the salty air. To me the smell of fish was good because I had been brought up with it. Papa's hands and clothes smelled of fish, no matter how much he washed.

Whap! The teacher hit my knuckles with the ruler. My hand stung. He snatched away my picture and scrunched it up.

"Pay attention, Hendrik," said the teacher. "You are here to learn."

He took out the map of Europe, where 'Germany' was written in bold black letters wherever Germany had invaded. 'Germany' was written over top of 'Holland'. Where was my beloved country? But nobody objected. So I did. "Sir?"

"Yes, Hendrik?"

"I'm proud to be Dutch."

The teacher scowled. "You will write on the board fifty times that you are proud to be German."

"No, sir, I will not," I said, defiantly.

"Go straight to the principal's office." He scribbled out a note. "Give this to the principal."

I gathered up my books and headed out the door to the principal's office, fearing the worst punishment.

* * *

CHAPTER 12

THE ORGAN GRINDER

I SPENT THE REST OF THE AFTERNOON sitting in the principal's office. Speaking out was getting me nowhere, but how could I remain silent? There was nothing left for me to learn in this school of lies.

The principal finally called me into his office. I handed him the note explaining why I was here. He read it. "Hmm," he muttered. "What if I told you that I agree with you completely?"

My eyes flew open. "You do?"

"Absolutely. But these are terrible times. The Nazis run the school now, not me. I am a puppet on a string. I have to do whatever they tell me. If I don't listen, I'll lose my job and no other school will be allowed to hire me. I have a wife and five children, so I must obey. Until..."

"Until when?" I interrupted.

"Until Holland rids itself of these German intruders and we regain our own country once again."

"When will that be?" I asked.

"I do not know. I hope soon. Hendrik, never forget that all people are created equal. And never forget that you are

Dutch. But for a while we must play along with the Germans. For just a little while."

"Yes, sir."

"Now go home."

Who would have thought that going to the principal's office would turn out to be a good thing? I felt a lot better. I didn't have to be asked to leave a second time. I hurried out of the school. Inside the school the air smelled stale, but outside the air beckoned me as it blew from the sea. I took a big breath, inhaled then exhaled. I whistled as I walked through the schoolyard. It was recess again and, just my bad luck, Eric and his gang cornered me. Soon the taunts of "Jew-lover" followed me.

I ignored my tormenters as I turned away, trying to walk tall and full of confidence. Eric sized me up and called his goons off. I let out my breath. I hadn't realized that I was holding it. I left the schoolyard, grateful to be in one piece, and headed for home.

Something shiny on the road caught my eye and I picked it up. What luck, a coin! I thought of all the wonderful things I could buy to eat and my mouth watered. Or maybe I would go to the cinema.

As I looked around my neighborhood, everything seemed wrong. Where was the usual bustle of merchants and the traffic of cars and cyclists? Where were all the shoppers and pedestrians? Where were the mothers and children playing in the park? Even the shutters on houses were closed. Then I had my answer. An oncoming procession of soldiers and tanks had scared everyone away. My safe and beautiful neighborhood looked foreign as the soldiers marched by. The commander shouted orders at them and they raised their arms in the air. They looked menacing as they took up the whole road. I needed to keep on moving. I hurried into the library and watched from behind the window. When the procession finally marched out of sight, people slowly came back to the street, like they did after a rainstorm. The street became alive again.

Soon the music from the organ grinder with the monkey entertained a small crowd. I came out to watch the monkey doing flips. It made me laugh out loud. We applauded. A couple of angry looking soldiers worked their way to the front of the crowd. The music came suddenly to a halt as the organ grinder was kicked and punched by these soldiers because he had a yellow cloth star sewn on the outside of his coat.

This was another new and hateful law that the Nazis had introduced. The yellow Star of David branded them as Jews so they could be easily recognized. The penalty for not wearing the star was six months in jail and a large fine. We had heard that people were tortured in the jails and sometimes killed.

The organ grinder fell to the ground and the monkey screeched, jumped off the music box, and stroked the man's head with his paw. The monkey had more compassion than the soldiers. The man winced with pain as he held his sore ribs and struggled to his feet. I breathed a sigh of relief. He was going to be all right.

I fingered the coin in my pocket and said goodbye to my treat. As I passed the monkey, I put my coin into its tin can. The monkey did a little dance for me and the organ grinder nodded his thanks.

* * *

CHAPTER 13
RUNNING AWAY TO SEA

I NEEDED AIR. MY HEAD WAS REELING. The image of the soldiers beating up the organ grinder haunted me. I needed to get away from it all. The only thing that I knew that could make me feel better was to go out in our boat. I headed straight for the wharf, looking for Papa. When I got to the boat, I called out to him, but there was no answer. I boarded the *Freedom* and took a look around in case he didn't hear me. He was nowhere to be found. I scratched my head. Maybe he was off selling his day's catch or maybe he was out buying supplies. I sat and waited impatiently. I paced back and forth. I just had to get out of here or I would explode. I felt like a shaken bottle of seltzer water.

What if I took the boat out myself for just a little while? Papa wouldn't even miss it. I knew how to steer the boat. Papa had always been beside me, but I could do it without him.

I started the motor and put it in reverse. Usually Papa stayed at the steering wheel, while I untied the boat. It was tricky doing both things myself. The more I hurried, the more I fumbled trying to untie the knots in the ropes on shore. The moment the boat was untied, it started backing up. When I looked up, I was horrified to find that the boat was heading straight toward another fishing boat. If anything happened to Papa's boat, not only would my name be mud, but also Papa wouldn't be able to make a living. And it would be all my fault.

I raced to the steering wheel and slipped in a puddle on the deck, landing hard on my left knee. My pants were torn and my knee was scraped, but no time for that because it looked as though I was going to crash. The owner yelled at me. When he saw that I was not changing my course, his anger turned to fear. He tried desperately to pull up his anchor, so that he could move his boat out of the way.

Gasping for air, I grabbed the steering wheel and yanked it hard with a silent prayer. I just missed hitting the boat by a whisker. The owner shook his fist at me. I was not going to wait to hear what he had to say. Instead I pulled quickly away.

Leaving the safety of the harbor, I headed out to sea, just like I had with Papa so many times.

A deep breath of salty sea air calmed me down right away. I headed out to one of Papa's favorite fishing spots, about two hours from shore. There I dropped anchor and took out my fishing rod from the cupboard and baited my hook. This was Papa's lucky spot and I pulled in one fish after another. I was feeling pretty good. I put my prizes into an empty barrel. This was the life. This is where I belonged. I had caught dinner for Mama and she would be proud.

My enjoyment was short-lived as doubts began to fill my head. Papa would be furious at me for taking the boat without permission. If I returned it now, he would never know. But how would I explain to Mama about the fish that I had caught for dinner? Papa would certainly notice that the fuel in the tank was down from the last time he had taken it out. And I had no money to refill the tank. My heart sank. I was in trouble.

The wind picked up and the boat rocked from side to side. Then it occurred to me. Why wasn't Papa out in the boat this afternoon? It was too early to take his fish to market. I looked around. Where were all the other fishing boats? I shivered from the cold and the realization that a storm was approaching. This was why Papa hadn't gone out. This was why there were no other fishing boats out. I pulled up my collar. The wind increased and the swelling waves bounced the boat around. Water splashed over the deck soaking me to the bone. I had a raincoat down below, but I didn't dare leave the steering wheel to find it while the sea was this rough.

Fear spurred me on. I had better hurry back. I wasn't that far out. I pulled up anchor and headed for the protection of the harbor. Once more, I looked at my catch and smiled, but the smile left my lips as the waves washed the deck. "My fish," I cried, as I watched the barrel of fish tumble overboard.

I tried to turn the steering wheel and head for the harbor. To my alarm, I couldn't control the wheel. The high winds and the strong current pushed the boat in the opposite direction from where I was trying to steer. My hands and arms ached as I fought with the wheel. Suddenly the boat tilted sideways, sending me crashing to the deck. My right knee was scraped and bleeding. And now I saw dorsal fins circling the boat. I gulped as I looked down at my bleeding knee. Could the sharks smell my blood? The fog was rolling in on me. Was I going to be shipwrecked and suffer the same fate as my Uncle Stefan?

There was only one thing to do. I sent out an emergency message on our wireless radio to any boat close enough to pick it up. "May Day! May Day!" I kept repeating the signal for trouble.

"Come in," the radio cracked. "This is *Mermaid*. Give me your latitude and longitude. Over."

I groaned. Why hadn't I paid more attention in geography class? "I don't know how to do that," I said.

"You're a kid?"

"Yes."

"How long have you been at sea?"

I looked at my watch. "I travelled west and anchored about two hours from the wharf."

"What's your boat's name?"

"*Freedom.*"

"Nice name."

"Wait, something's wrong," I yelled into the radio. "The motor just stopped."

"Don't panic. I'm not too far away. Try to start the boat. Are you wearing a life jacket?"

"Yes," I answered as I tried the motor again, but it wouldn't catch. The wind kept pushing the boat in the wrong direction.

"It won't restart and I'm going sideways and there are sharks!"

"Switch on your lights, *Freedom*, and keep beeping your horn."

Silence. "*Mermaid*, are you there?" No one answered. "*Mermaid?*" I called. Still no answer. My hands were blue and stiff from the cold, but I switched on the lights and honked my horn. 'Don't let the wind swallow the sound,' I prayed. The waves covered the first deck. One of Papa's nets washed over. Oh, no, I had forgotten to tie it down. Papa would be furious.

The sharks kept circling the boat. I waited. At least someone had heard my cry for help.

* * *

CHAPTER 14

RESCUE

THE *FREEDOM* TIPPED SIDEWAYS. I grabbed the railing and held on for dear life. "A good captain always goes down with his ship," I said to the wind, "Goodbye my good friend, Pieter. Don't forget me. Goodbye, Mama. Cry for me. Goodbye, Papa. I'm sorry about the *Freedom*. I'm sorry about everything." My tears blended with the salt of the seawater coming at me from all sides. I gulped in air and hiccupped.

"Ahoy!" called a voice, over the sounds of the crashing waves.

I was so startled that my hiccups disappeared. "Ahoy," I called back. "Over here!" I honked the horn.

Soon a man tied his boat to my boat and climbed aboard. The captain of the *Mermaid*, dressed in a yellow slicker, rain hat, and boots, looked like an experienced and weathered seaman.

"Thank you, thank you for saving me," I kept repeating.

The fisherman ruffled my hair. "You're a brave one to be out at sea alone on such a stormy day. There must be a good story here, but first let's get your boat tied tightly to mine. I'll tow her in. Then you'll tell me your tale in my dry cabin."

I nodded my head in gratitude.

He quickly secured a rope from his boat to mine. We boarded the *Mermaid* and he started towing. He didn't say much until we reached the safety of the harbor. Then he invited me into his captain's quarters. My teeth were chattering.

"Take this blanket and warm yourself."

I wrapped the wool blanket around me and sat down.

"Here's a drink."

I took a gulp and started to choke on the strong coffee. He laughed a hearty laugh. "My coffee is not for the faint-hearted. But I can see you are chilled, through and through. This should warm your innards. Take another sip. Slowly, now."

I took another sip and warmed my hands on the mug.

"Tell me your tale."

"Not much to tell," I began. "I really wanted to go fishing, but Papa wasn't around. I thought I could take her out on my own."

"Didn't you hear about the storm coming from the north?"

I shook my head.

"That's probably why your father wasn't out fishing. You had a close call and I'm not just talking about your boat sinking."

"What are you talking about?" I asked.

"I found you heading southwest toward the English Channel."

I gasped. "The current pulled me out that far?"

The fisherman nodded. "You were heading into waters that are heavily patrolled by the Germans. German warships and police patrol boats guard the sea borders between England and Germany's occupied territories. You're lucky that I found you before they did."

I gulped. What was the fisherman doing in an area that was so heavily patrolled? He must be hiding something, I thought, but it was none of my business. I considered myself lucky that he was out there to save me. "Thank you," I said again, as we approached the wharf.

"That must be your father, that man pacing back and forth at the dock."

I borrowed his binoculars and nodded. "That's him. And, boy, does he look angry."

* * *

CHAPTER 15
BIG TROUBLE

WHEN WE LANDED AT THE DOCK, Papa hugged me so hard that I felt crushed. He thanked the fisherman and pulled out money to give him a reward. The fisherman put up his hand to stop him. "I was just helping another person in need," he said. "Keep your money. I'm glad that your son is all right. He's a good boy. He was plenty scared out there, but I think he learned his lesson." The fisherman tipped his rain hat and headed for a nearby café.

Papa raised his voice and shook a finger at me. "What did you think you were doing?"

"I just wanted to go fishing and you weren't around to take me."

"Your mother is beside herself with worry. When I got home, she said that you never came home from school. So I checked at Pieter's house, but you weren't there either. So I decided to check the wharf. And what do I find? My boat is gone!"

"I'm sorry, Papa." I couldn't look him in the eye.

"How could you be so reckless? I came in early because of the storm coming this way. How could you think of taking my boat out alone?"

"I thought..."

"You weren't thinking, Hendrik. I taught you to read the wind and the waves. Why didn't you come back in?"

"It was calm when I first went out and as soon as the storm hit, I headed for the docks. But the wind caught me and I couldn't get back." I shivered.

"Let's get you home," Papa said, putting his coat on me. "I did some stupid things, too, when I was a boy. Like the time I tried to jump on a moving train and missed. Luckily, just my pride was hurt."

I smiled gratefully at Papa for forgiving me.

Mama took one look at me and started in. "How could you worry us like this? Look at your knees. You're bleeding! Let me clean you up. And you're shivering. Papa, start boiling the water. Hendrik needs a good soak."

I winced as Mama cleaned my wounds. "There's a brave boy." She kissed me on the forehead. "Help Papa fill the tub with hot water."

I lugged bucket after bucket of boiling water. Mama added cold water until she announced, "It's just right."

I put my big toe in. "Ouch."

"Get in," ordered Mama.

Mama held a towel up and looked away as I climbed into the tin tub. I felt like a lobster boiling, but I didn't complain. It was good to be alive.

My eyes got heavy as I soaked. So much had happened today. I yawned and sank into the soapy water.

"Out with you," called Mama. "You'll turn into a prune."
She startled me awake.

"Get some sleep. You're going to need it because this house
needs a scrubbing from top to bottom."

"Yes, Mama." She left me a towel and walked away. I
wrapped the soft warm towel around me and headed for bed.

As I closed my eyes, the eye of a shark seemed to stare at
me and I sprang up with my heart pounding. Yes, I was very
lucky. Tonight, I slept with the teddy bear of my childhood.
Just for tonight, I thought. I held it close to me. My bed felt
as though it were rocking, back and forth. I ran to the sink and
threw up. Mama tucked me in again and stroked my hair until
I started to nod off to sleep.

*The shark chased me all over the boat. Suddenly he turned
into a Nazi soldier. He gained on me and I screamed.*

Papa hurried to my side. It was the middle of the night.
He held my hand until my eyes were heavy once more.

* * *

CHAPTER 16
MITZVAH

THE NEXT MORNING, I woke up with a terrible headache. Yesterday's wild adventure at sea came flooding back to me. When I tried to sit up, I groaned.

Mama greeted me with a mop. I wanted to hide beneath the covers. "Get up and get to work."

"But I'm sick."

Mama felt my forehead. "You're fine."

"What about breakfast?" I asked.

"Have some toast, then, and hurry up about it."

I poured myself some milk and slowly buttered my toast, trying to delay the inevitable. Papa came in, face unshaven. "Hendrik, want some eggs?"

"Yes, please," I said, eagerly.

Mama placed the mop beside me, in case I should forget. She frowned at Papa who cracked eggs into a pan. "You're spoiling that boy."

Papa scrambled the eggs. "He's going to need lots of energy today to help me."

"I thought Hendrik was going to work for me all day," complained Mama.

"Hey, don't fight over me," I joked. They both ignored me.

"Hendrik, needs to come down to the wharf with me this morning," said Papa.

"What?" exclaimed Mama. "You're going to reward him for what he did by taking him fishing?"

"No, of course not, dear," Papa said kindly. "Hendrik is going to do what the Jewish people call a mitzvah."

"What's a mitzvah, Papa?"

"It's the act of doing something good without expecting anything back in return, like money or a reward."

I look at him puzzled.

"Hendrik, the fisherman helped you. In return, I want you to give him your time. Today, you are going to paint his boat without pay. This will be your way to thank the fisherman who saved our boat and, more important, your neck."

"Oh, I see," I said. This mitzvah made a lot of sense to me. It was way better than scrubbing floors all day. Things were looking a lot brighter. Papa made the best eggs. "Seconds please."

Mama shook her head, but Papa smiled and cracked another egg with one hand over the pan. "Papa, you could give up fishing and become a chef."

"I almost had to, when you nearly sank the *Freedom*. But who would come to a restaurant with only eggs on the menu?"

I smiled and scraped up the rest of my eggs with my toast.

The paint cans were heavy as we lugged everything down to the docks. The *Mermaid* was tied up. That friendly, weathered fisherman was getting his boat ready for the day.

"Good morning," called my father.

The fisherman waved and invited us on board.

"In all the rush yesterday to get Hendrik warm and dry, I never got your name," said Papa.

"Friends just call me Old Sea Dog."

Papa laughed and shook his hand.

"What's with all the paints and brushes?" asked Old Sea Dog.

"Hendrik came up with a perfect idea," lied Papa. "He wants to paint your boat to thank you for saving him yesterday."

"That's mighty kind of your boy, but as you can see, I was just heading out to sea."

"Not if I'm buying you a hearty meal this morning," said Papa.

Old Sea Dog smiled. "Now that's an offer I can't refuse." Papa and the fisherman headed off to the restaurant and left me standing there on my own.

* * *

CHAPTER 17
RECRUITING

I HAD AN IDEA. All the Jewish kids had no school and nothing to do all day. Surely they would love to help me. Maybe when we were done and the paint was dry, Old Sea Dog could take us all fishing.

I left the paint on board and ran to the Jewish section. Luckily, there were no bullies or Nazis around to give me trouble. Probably too early. First, I knocked on Pieter's door. He came to the door in his nightshirt.

"Are you sick, Pieter?"

"No." He rubbed his eyes.

"Why aren't you dressed?" I asked.

"What's the point? I have nowhere to go." Pieter yawned.

"Yes you do," I said.

"I do?" he asked.

"I need your help to paint Old Sea Dog's boat."

"Why?"

"He saved my life."

Pieter was wide awake now. "Who's Old Sea Dog and what happened?"

"Get dressed and meet me at the docks. I've got to get

Malka and Jacob. I'll tell you all the story later."

"Don't leave me in suspense," said Pieter.

"Later," I called as I hurried off.

When I reached Malka's family bakery, her older sister was busy serving a customer. I waved and climbed the stairs to my friend's apartment. Out of breath, I knocked at the door. Malka's father answered. "Hello, Hendrik. Good to see you. Shouldn't you be in school?" he asked.

"Papa has some chores for me today. Do you think that Malka could help me?"

"Malka's in the kitchen baking the bread with her mother. I think she's pretty busy."

I had to speak to her, so I blew our secret whistle. Two short, one long.

Malka came running to the front door wearing an apron with flour all over her hands. "Hello Hendrik."

She looked beautiful even with flour all over her. I sighed. "Can you help us paint a boat?"

"Can I, Father? Please? I haven't been out all week."

"But your mother needs you..."

I interrupted. "Excuse me, sir, but I'm doing this as a mitzvah."

Malka's father smiled. "A gentile boy knows what mitzvah means?"

"Yes, sir. Helping without repayment," I said, proudly.

He laughed. "Malka, go, help your friend do this mitzvah."

"Thank you, Father." She kissed him on the cheek and untied her apron. Then she grabbed my hand and pulled me out the door before her father could change his mind.

We headed toward Jacob's house. His father was tutoring him in English at the kitchen table. I asked his father, "Can Jacob join us to paint a boat?"

"Please?" Jacob begged.

"He must learn English because we are leaving for Canada where we have a cousin. Our cousin writes that in Canada Jacob would be allowed to go to school and we won't be persecuted because we are Jewish."

"Please? It would only be for a short time. Afterwards, Jacob can go back to his studies," I argued.

"I don't think so," said Jacob's father.

"But we're doing a mitzvah," I said.

He gave a belly laugh. "A mitzvah, you say?"

I nodded my head.

"You may go, Jacob. We'll continue our English classes later."

The word mitzvah seemed to have magical powers. We wasted no time and headed for the docks.

* * *

CHAPTER 18
TEAMWORK

WE GOT TO THE DOCKS WHERE PIETER was already waiting for us.

"What's this really about?" Pieter asked.

"I took my father's boat out yesterday, without permission," I said.

"Alone?" asked Malka.

"Yes," I answered.

"Are you nuts?" asked Pieter.

"Go on," encouraged Jacob.

"A fierce storm came in and blew me out to sea. A shark tried to eat me and Old Sea Dog saved my neck."

Malka gasped.

Jacob's eyes popped. "Then what happened?"

I was having so much fun being with my friends that I almost forgot about the dangers of the street. Suddenly I became alert, remembering that there were Nazi soldiers near every corner. I stopped and looked around. "Soldiers, coming this way," I whispered. "Hurry, hide the yellow stars. Turn your coats inside out. Follow my lead."

As the soldiers got closer, I spoke loudly, "Those stupid

Jewish pigs. Let's find us some and beat them up."

"Yeah," chimed in Pieter.

"Let's steal their coats and let them freeze to death," said Malka.

The soldiers heard this and smiled to one another as they walked past us.

"Don't run," I whispered. We walked faster now. "Our little play acting worked." I breathed a sigh of relief. We didn't relax again until we were safely on the *Mermaid*. "Let me finish my story," I said. "We were rudely interrupted." So I started my story again about my solo trip out to sea.

"My knee was bleeding and the sharks were circling. There must have been dozens of them," I exaggerated. "But this one shark was bigger than the rest, and he had his eye on me."

My story got bigger and bigger like the fish that got away, but I had a captive audience and they were swallowing it hook, line, and sinker. The story continued as we all picked up paintbrushes and began to paint the *Mermaid*.

"Here, I am holding onto the railing, bleeding, and the killer shark, snapping its jaws, jumps on my boat and comes right at me. But I give it a mighty kick and stab it with my knife, right in the eye. It never even had a chance."

"Oh, my," said Malka admiringly.

For extra impact, I showed them my cut knee. The boys looked very impressed and Malka looked away with her hand over her mouth.

I noticed a loose board on the *Mermaid*'s deck and went below to look for a hammer. Then I came across some crates. "Hey, come below," I called.

My friends came down.

"Look at all these crates," said Pieter.

I peeked into a crate. "Hey, over here." My friends gathered round. "This lid is broken and look at all the cans and jars in here." We started pulling out jam jars, cans of soup, and beans.

"I haven't seen this much food since before the war," said Jacob.

I sifted through the crate. "Pickles!" I grabbed jar and twisted the lid until it opened. "I'll just have one." I popped it into my mouth and pickle juice dribbled down my chin. I loved the sour taste. "Mmm. Just one more."

"You're going to be in trouble," said Malka.

"Give me one," said Pieter. I handed him a pickle and he licked his lips.

"Encore," said Jacob. He crunched the pickle loudly, and then grabbed another one.

"You're all going to be in trouble," said Malka.

"Too late now, only one left. You might as well take it." I held out the jar to her.

Malka couldn't resist and popped it into her mouth. She chewed slowly to savor the taste. "You'd better tell Old Sea Dog."

"No way," I said.

"If you don't, I will," she said.

"Fine." I shoved my hands into my pockets.

I found a hammer and fixed the loose board. Then we all got to work and painted the boat. "Do you realize that we haven't all been together since you were kicked out of school?" I asked. Then I sneezed and splattered paint all over my face, making everyone laugh.

With four of us working, we got the job done pretty quickly. Before we knew it, Papa and Old Sea Dog came to inspect our work. Papa looked surprised to see my friends helping me. "How did you talk your friends into doing your work? Hmm?"

"We wanted to help," said Malka.

The others all murmured in agreement.

"Nice job," said Old Sea Dog. "The *Mermaid* was in need of a paint job."

I shifted from foot to foot. Malka pushed me forward. "Okay, okay," I muttered under my breath. I cleared my throat. "I found all these crates in the lower deck and one of them was broken. I saw that it was filled with all kinds of canned food. Since the war and food rationing, I just don't see these kinds of food any more. I hope that you don't mind, but I really love pickles. I opened a jar, but I only meant to eat one pickle. Then I had one more and one more. And then I had to share it with my friends. I don't have any money, but I'll work to pay for the pickles," I said, all in one breath.

I was ready for a lecture from Papa, but instead he looked at Old Sea Dog with his eyebrows raised. "So that's why you were coming from the English Channel when you saved my son. You were smuggling food."

Old Sea Dog shrugged. "What can I say? I'm a businessman who imports and exports food, but since the war, I have to smuggle it to England to make a living. It's a dangerous business, but there's good money in it. There's quite a demand for this food and I seem to thrive on danger."

"Don't worry, Old Sea Dog. Your secret stays with us. We aren't going to tell, are we children? Hmm?"

"No, sir," we said in chorus.

"Remember children, these are dangerous times and Old Sea Dog saved Hendrik's life. Not a word. Let's shake on it." Papa solemnly shook each of our hands.

"Papa, can you take us out fishing, now that we're done?"

"I have to buy a new net. You lost the other one, remember?" Papa chided me.

"I'm sorry about the net. Please, can Old Sea Dog take us out in our boat while the paint on his boat dries?" I asked, boldly.

"I don't mind," said Old Sea Dog. "I could catch me some dinner."

Papa's face softened. "If you're sure that it's no bother."

"No trouble at all," said Old Sea Dog.

Before Papa could change his mind, we all boarded the *Freedom* and took off.

* * *

CHAPTER 19

MERMAID

THE STORM HAD PASSED AND THE SEA WAS CALM. In the past, Pieter and Jacob both had come fishing with me. But this was a new adventure for Malka. She was so excited and wanted to know everything about the boat. I took pleasure in teaching her. She sure smelled nice, like freshly baked bread.

Jacob interrupted. "Hendrik, give me a hand."

I put worms on my friends' hooks. Malka turned pale when I stabbed the worm with the hook. "Let me show you how to cast." I pulled in a fish too small to keep, but she looked so impressed that I put it into the bucket of water. Fortunately, I caught a keeper next, so I threw the small one back when Malka wasn't looking.

"Did I ever tell you about how my boat got its name?" asked Old Sea Dog.

"Tell us," we all said together.

Old Sea Dog lit his pipe and took a puff. The smoke swirled from his mouth.

"One day, long ago, when I was just a boy, I heard singing in the mist. That could only mean one thing."

He paused, while we all asked, "What?"

"Mermaids. Lonely mermaids sit on rocks combing their long hair, singing to lure fishermen to the rocks. Their boats hit the rocks and sink. When the fishermen begin to drown, the mermaids save them, giving them the kiss of life. But in return, they must remain under the sea forever as mermen."

"Then how come you're still here?" Pieter asked.

"I heard singing, but I knew about the fate of those who followed the beautiful voices. This time the voice was not so beautiful. The song was sad and forlorn. In my nets, amongst the fish, I had accidentally caught a mermaid. Her tail was emerald green, her hair long and blond. I listened carefully to the words of her song. She sang of swimming free and returning to her kingdom below. She promised to bring me pearls from the clams and sunken treasures lost at sea, to make me a rich man, if only I would set her free.

"'I will free you,' I said, 'but not for coins or jewels. Protect me and my boat forever. That is what I ask for.'

"She agreed and I set her free. She flicked her tail and the other mermaids came to embrace her. Then, in an instant, they were gone. I'm an old man now, and I have been out at sea almost every day of my life and have never been shipwrecked. Sometimes, on a misty night, I can hear the song of a mermaid. That is why I called my boat, the *Mermaid*."

Suddenly Malka's fishing rod began to move and bend. "I caught a fish," she shouted.

Old Sea Dog talked her through it. "Give her more line, that's it. Reel her in slowly. Not jerky, take your time." He grabbed a net and helped her land the cod. "Not the biggest I've seen, but a decent size to be sure. Certainly the most special, because it's your first fish. Take it home for dinner. You've done yourself proud, young lady."

Malka beamed. We kept her fish in the barrel and she spent the ride home, watching over it.

"Shhh," whispered Old Sea Dog. "Did you hear that?"

"Hear what?" I asked.

"That singing."

I stared into the waves. I could have sworn that I, too, heard soft singing.

"I heard it too," said Jacob in a whisper.

"It was just the wind," said Pieter.

"Was it?" asked Old Sea Dog, smiling.

* * *

CHAPTER 20
QUICK ESCAPE

PAPA AND I WENT TO BUY BREAD from Malka's family bakery. They made the best bread in Amsterdam.

"Hendrik, you're growing like a weed."

"I'm fourteen, Mr. Mendel."

"Time flies. I can't believe two years have gone by since the Nazis invaded Holland."

"Where's Malka?"

"Upstairs. It's safer for her to stay at home. Take a poppy seed cookie, Hendrik. I'm sorry that it isn't as sweet as I used to make it. Sugar is so hard to come by."

I munched on my cookie. "It's yummy."

Mr. Mendel smiled and gave me a second cookie.

"Thank you, Mr. Mendel."

Papa bought pumpernickel bread. "Go on Hendrik. Visit your friend, upstairs, while Mr. Mendel and I have a chat."

I ran upstairs and knocked on the door. When Malka saw me, her face lit up. "Hi, Hendrik. Come on in."

I greeted Mrs. Mendel as I took off my coat. "My mother wants to know how you are doing."

"Not so good, I'm afraid. These are terrible times," said Mrs. Mendel.

I nodded, because I didn't know what else to say.

Malka grabbed my hand and led me to the sofa. "I'm glad you came. I've been so lonely. Our fishing trip seems so long ago. I want to feel the fresh air in my face again." She sighed. "Mama won't let me go outside any more because she's too afraid. You have to tell me everything that's happening outside."

I stared at Malka's hair. She had the prettiest hair, all dark ringlets. Whenever she moved, they bounced around her face.

"Well?" prodded Malka.

"School is all lies. It's what you hear on the radio and read in the newspapers. Even our textbooks have changed. They're all about German history and say nothing about the rest of the world. It's as if the Germans erased our history. I can't stand it. I never used to skip school, but now I do all the time. Thank goodness, my parents understand and let me go fishing. Mama and Papa are also angry at what is being taught."

"What else?" asked Malka.

"I'm angry and disappointed with my classmates. Nobody questions anything and they just do what they are told."

"How's Hans?" she asked.

I took a deep breath. I knew that she had a crush on him, but I had to tell her the truth. I scratched my chin like Papa did when he was thinking. "Hans only talks about joining the Youth Nazi Party. He finds it exciting and glamorous."

"Oh." Malka sunk deeper into the sofa. "I thought he liked me and I'm Jewish."

"I'm sorry, Malka, but he's been brainwashed. You're not a person to him. As far as Hans is concerned, the Jews are the reason for all of our country's problems. Hitler blames everything on the Jews." When she took my hand, I started to sweat.

"What about your other friends, Ger and Josef?" asked Malka. "Do they want to join the Youth Nazi Party too?"

"Ger hates what's happening to the Jews, but he's too afraid to speak out, ever since..."

"Ever since what?" Malka asked.

"Ever since Josef tried to stop a soldier from beating up a little Jewish girl and her mother on the street. The Nazi soldier arrested him and his entire family. Nobody has seen or heard from them since," I said, sadly.

"I've heard some terrible news, too."

"What?" I asked.

"Jews aren't allowed to own radios. But we have one hidden. The Germans feed us propaganda. They only brag that they are winning the war and that they have few casualties. But our radio gets the radio broadcasts from England, and the Germans aren't always doing as well as they claim. Do you want to hear what's really happening?"

I nodded.

Malka gave me this mischievous look and she pulled a radio out from behind the sofa. She turned it on low and we sat close together listening. Her leg brushed against mine and it was hard to concentrate on the news report.

The announcer said, "The Nazis have stormed the hospitals and killed the mentally and physically handicapped. They are killing anyone who is different, including homosexuals. They are arresting and shooting Jehovah's Witnesses because they refused to serve in Hitler's army or salute him."

"Malka?" called Mrs. Mendel.

"Yes, Mother?"

"I need your help with the bread."

"Coming in a minute." Malka turned off the radio and tucked it back safely behind the sofa. "I'm so afraid, Hendrik. Jews aren't safe here. Every day things are getting worse for the Jews. The Nazis tell the Jews that they are being sent to labor camps, but they are lying. They are also arresting children, the sick, and the old. We need to escape from Holland. Papa and Mama talk a lot about going to Palestine."

"Where is Palestine?" I asked.

"It's far away, in the Middle East."

"Why there?" I asked.

"You've heard of the prophet Abraham?"

"Yes, we learned that in Sunday school," I said.

"The Lord ordered Abraham, who was the first Jew, to go to the land that is now called Palestine. It is the ancestral home of the Jews and that's why my family wants to go there."

"I'll miss you if you go, Malka."

"I'll miss you too, Hendrik." Malka pecked me on the cheek and I blushed. "Let me walk you downstairs."

"And where do you think you are going, young lady?" asked Mrs. Mendel, as we approached the stairs.

"I'll help you in a minute, Mother. I'm just walking Hendrik downstairs to the bakery."

"No, you stay upstairs where it is safe."

"But, Mother..."

"No, buts. Thank you for visiting, Hendrik. Say hello to your mother from me." She handed me my coat and I waved goodbye to Malka. I went back downstairs to the bakery where Papa was busy talking with Mr. Mendel.

"Did you have a nice visit?" asked Mr. Mendel.

"Yes, sir."

"It's nice of you to come. Malka misses her friends," said Mr. Mendel.

I was about to say something to him, when there was a commotion at the door. Soldiers in Nazi uniforms stormed into the bakery. They shouted orders and, when Mr. Mendel protested, they kicked and punched him and threw him to the floor. He moaned and I covered my ears. I gave a silent scream, "No..."

I was glued to the spot. This couldn't be real.

Papa pulled me away and we dashed out the back door. Papa never let go of my hand as we ran through the winding alleys. Where was he taking me?

Poor Mr. Mendel. Poor Malka when she finds out. Will she be safe upstairs?

I was gasping for breath, but Papa never slowed down. He

tugged on my arm to go faster. I quickly looked behind me. "Papa, nobody's chasing us," I gasped.

Papa kept running, as though he were being chased by the devil.

Now I knew where we were going, as I saw the shipping docks in the distance. As soon as we got to the wharf, I helped Papa launch our fishing boat as fast as possible.

I didn't feel safe until we were out at sea. Then I started to shake. Papa didn't say a word, but he put his arms around me. I was surprised that Papa was shaking too and I hugged him back.

* * *

CHAPTER 21
THE FISH THAT GOT AWAY

PAPA PULLED THE PUMPERNICKEL out from his coat pocket and offered me some bread. My tummy rumbled, but I was too upset to eat. The bread reminded me of Mr. Mendel.

"Hendrik, I owe you an explanation for why we ran."

"You were scared?" I asked.

"Of course, I was scared and I was worried about you." Papa shifted from one foot to another. "I had no choice. We were outnumbered by the soldiers and they had guns. If we had tried to help Mr. Mendel, the Nazis would have shot us. Plain and simple. I'm not proud of myself — that I couldn't help my friend — and I'm not proud that I ran away. Sometimes, you can help and other times you can just make things worse. It was one of those other times. But now that it's over, I will go back and, if it's too late, " his voice choked, "I will help his family in any way that I can."

I nodded. I knew that my father was not a coward. I understand that he did what he thought was best at the time. I tried to block the memory of the soldiers beating up Mr. Mendel.

When Papa stopped the motor, I heaved out the anchor.

With a flick of his wrist, Papa cast his line.

My line tangled and Papa automatically fixed it. His hands felt like leather, as they wrapped around mine. Together, we cast the line far out into the sea.

Fishing always calmed me down. I made myself comfortable and sat on a chair, kicked off my wooden clogs and comfortably held my fishing rod as I stared out to sea. It was a beautiful, sunny day and I closed my eyes in the sunlight. It was so peaceful out here. Why did people have to go to war? Why did they hate other people just because they were different?

Suddenly, the roar of a motor interrupted my thoughts. My heart started to race as I saw a patrol boat approaching us.

"Stop and let me board," shouted the soldier.

"Keep fishing," Papa said to me under his breath.

The soldier climbed aboard. He looked young and full of himself. He strutted around our boat sneering at us.

"Papers!" he demanded.

Papa always had our identity cards on hand. He took them from his pocket and handed them over.

"They seem in order." The soldier sounded disappointed.

My fishing rod bent. "I've got a bite!"

Papa ignored the soldier and helped me. "A codfish. She's a big one. Hang on tight." He lifted the net and scooped up the fish. "She's a beauty. You're a fine fisherman, Hendrik."

The soldier grabbed my fish. "I'll take that." The fish flopped in his arms. He didn't even have the sense to hit the fish over the head. "Catch yourself another one," he demanded.

I started to reach out to take my fish back, but Papa hugged me close so I couldn't make a move.

All I could hope was that the soldier would get into trouble because his uniform was dirty and stank of fish.

The fish squirmed and fell to the wet floor of our boat. I could easily have grabbed it, but I did nothing to stop it from sliding over the side of the boat and back into the water. Good! He didn't deserve my fish. "Too bad he got away," I said, trying not to smile.

"Catch me another one," he demanded.

Papa winked at me and I knew what he was thinking.

I put my fishing rod in without any bait. After a while, the soldier got impatient and stormed off.

We watched silently as his boat disappeared from sight. I baited my hook and immediately caught another fish.

Papa and I looked at each other and started to chuckle. We laughed until the tears fell down our faces. We were both thinking about the fish that got away.

* * *

CHAPTER 22
THE HOUSE OF CARDS

PAPA TOOK ME TO THE GOODMANS' FISH MARKET to sell his fish. Mr. and Mrs. Goodman gave me a hard candy. I put it in my mouth and sucked on the peppermint. Papa talked business with the Goodmans by the cash register.

When Pieter came in, we built a house of cards together in the back of the store. It took a very steady hand to place a card without knocking over all the other standing cards. When we finished the whole deck, I looked at our house of cards. Pretty impressive, I thought. Pieter stood up and swiped his hands through it, knocking it down.

"Hey," I yelled.

Pieter put his hands in his pockets and bowed his head.

"What's bothering you?" I asked.

Pieter shrugged. "I turned fourteen this week and everybody forgot."

I felt embarrassed. Pieter had remembered my fourteenth birthday and I had forgotten his. I felt in my pocket and pulled out my favorite pocketknife that I used for cutting rope on the boat. "Now you've ruined the surprise." I handed it to him. "Happy birthday!"

His face lit up. "Thanks, Hendrik. You're the best!"

As we spent the next hour rebuilding the house of cards, Pieter said, "Remember how we used to play at school everyday? It was bad enough when Jews weren't allowed to attend public schools and we had to start our own, but now the Germans put a stop to that too."

I interrupted. "I have some more bad news."

"What?" asked Pieter.

"Something horrible happened to Malka's father."

"Tell me," said Pieter.

"We were buying bread when Nazi soldiers came. They tried to close Mr. Mendel's bakery. When he argued with them, they kicked and punched him."

"That's awful," said Pieter. "Is Malka okay?"

Suddenly, a brick shattered the front window and we both dove for cover.

"Filthy Jews, leave town!" boomed a voice. We hid behind the counter and Papa and Pieter's father came running toward us. The voices moved away. Papa signalled us to stay put. He tiptoed over to the window, trying to avoid the broken glass, and peeked outside.

I looked over and saw that our house of cards was flattened. It took so long to build and it took nothing to tear it down.

We heard more glass breaking, but it was coming from next door. We waited until Papa motioned that it was all right to get up.

Mrs. Goodman cried, "What will become of us?" She took

her broom and started to sweep the glass into the dustpan. She looked shattered, like the glass.

"We have to go now," Papa announced.

We hurried down the street. All the Jewish stores on the street had been attacked. There was glass everywhere.

Papa took me straight home. He was angry and went to his workshop from where I heard banging. It was his way of dealing with his rage.

Mama nagged at me to take out the garbage. I was feeling edgy and didn't want to stay home. I grabbed the bag and took it out. But I didn't want to go back in. I decided to visit my neighbor Johan.

I knocked on the door. "Hello, Mr. Vandussan."

"Good to see you, Hendrik. Let me get Johan for you." I waited by the front door. "Johan," he called.

Johan came running down the stairs. "Hendrik. I'm so happy to see you. My brothers have been annoying me."

I laughed. "Do you want to play cards?"

"Come on," said Johan. "Let's go to my room, away from my brothers."

Johan shuffled the cards. He was so fast and smooth. Whenever I tried to shuffle, either none of the cards moved or all the cards flew everywhere. Johan dealt each of us seven cards, for a game of gin rummy. "My parents are very scared. They have become afraid to leave the house. Mr. Teitlebaum down the street went out to buy the newspaper and got taken away by the police. Nobody has seen him since. My parents make me keep up with my studies at home. My father lost his job because he is Jewish, so he is tutoring me. He is stricter than any of our teachers. You should see all the pages of math that I have to do and the essays that he makes me write. School was a vacation by comparison."

I played my card. Johan threw down a card and I picked it up. "Has your family thought about leaving Amsterdam?" I asked.

"Of course, but it's not so easy. My father tried to get a visa to Canada, but couldn't. So he paid a lot of money for fake passports." Johan's voice dropped to a whisper and I leaned forward to hear. "We know a family who went to Argentina and was turned back. Another went to Cuba and was turned back. No country wants us."

"Malka said her family was trying to escape to Palestine," I said, trying to be helpful.

Johan paced. "Yes, my parents also think that Palestine may be our only chance to survive. It is not easy. The British, who rule Palestine, aren't allowing Jewish immigration to Palestine. But there are ways to sneak in. My father has contacted a secret organization here in Amsterdam that has successfully smuggled in some Jews. They warned him that the ships that go to Palestine are not in very good shape. But as long as they float, we're willing to risk it." He put out three kings and four sixes. "Gin!"

"Want to play again?" I asked.

"No, I'm too anxious and my parents want to plan our

escape." I stood and Johan hugged me hard. "I may never see you again. We need to escape very soon or it will be too late."

I gulped. Too late? I dared not say these words out loud.

"Jews keep disappearing, never to be heard of again," Johan continued. "The police and soldiers are raiding Jewish homes and taking people away. We're running out of time. You've been a good friend, Hendrik, and I'll miss you."

"How will I know if you've gone to Palestine?" I asked.

Johan walked me outside to his front garden. "See this ace of spades?" He showed me the card. "If we leave in a hurry for Palestine, I'll hide, it…" Johan looked around, "…under this rock."

* * *

CHAPTER 23
CAPTURED

THE WIND WAS IN MY FACE as Papa and I headed off to sea. It was foggy, and Papa had to drive the boat slowly. He had to keep checking his compass, otherwise we might get lost in the fog. Seagulls flew above and behind the boat, following our good catch of fish on deck. I threw a small fish into the air and watched a seagull catch it as it fell. Other gulls cried out and tried to steal the fish away. The air smelled of salt, seaweed, and fish. I breathed in deeply and smiled. When I grew up, I wanted to be a fisherman, just like Papa. I would never have to go to school, do homework, or stay in for detentions. I would fish all day and it wouldn't seem like work.

A couple of hours passed. "Papa, where are we now?" I asked.

"You had better learn to read the compass yourself," said Papa. "Watch where the line moves on the compass. Tell me where we are heading."

"Halfway between north and west," I said.

"Yes, we are going northwest," said Papa. "And we're almost outside the Dutch territorial waters. Hendrik, do you know how to determine your position at sea in latitude and longitude and to read this marine chart?"

"No, Papa."

"I'd better teach you that, too."

Papa spent more than an hour teaching me how to figure my distance from shore landmarks, and use a compass to plot my position in degrees of latitude and longitude. I felt very proud when I got it right.

"Good work, Hendrik. Why don't you get us both a cup of tea from the thermos?"

I left Papa at the wheel and went over to the storage box to get the thermos. I thought I saw something move in the fog and looked up. Smack in front of us was a small boat. "Papa!" I yelled. But I was yelling against the wind and Papa would never hear me in time. I rushed to the bow and blew the foghorn. Papa looked up, startled. I pointed at the rowboat that we were about to crash into. Two people were rowing like mad, but not getting very far. Papa jerked the steering wheel to starboard, just missing the small craft.

Papa carefully pulled alongside the rowboat. "Are you crazy?" he called. "What are you doing so far out to sea in the fog without a light or a horn?" He stopped shouting when he saw their faces. A teenaged girl and a woman were rowing, while a little girl bailed out the water with a tin can. Their eyes were big as saucers and they looked frightened.

"Ah," he pulled on his chin. "You must be Jews. Are you trying to escape the Nazis in Holland? You have a long way to go."

"Please don't turn us in," pleaded the older girl.

"Of course not," said Papa. "But you'll never make it across the sea in that little broken down boat."

"Please help us," begged the girl.

Papa stroked his chin again while he was thinking. "Abandon your boat and come aboard mine. You're sinking."

The woman spoke for the first time. "My children and I are not going back to land until we reach England. It would mean sure death. The Nazis are looking for us in Holland. We are on their list of Jews."

"It's far too dangerous for you to go all the way across the North Sea in a rowboat with holes." Papa tried to talk sense into them.

"Then you can take us to England," said the woman, defiantly.

"For one thing, I don't have enough fuel. Two, I don't have a permit to leave Dutch waters. I would be stopped," Papa tried to explain.

"Then we decline your help, sir. Leave us and we will risk the lesser danger and try to cross the sea on our own," the woman declared.

Papa frowned. "I can't let you drown. Come back with me. I'll try somehow to arrange a better way of escape. But I'll need time."

"We have run out of time. Goodbye, sir. We will make it on our own." The woman was determined. She and her older daughter picked up their oars and started rowing away.

Papa sat down and held his head. "I don't know what to do."

A siren shrieked in the fog and we saw a patrol boat chase after the rowboat. Papa froze.

"What would have happened if the Jews had come aboard, Papa?" I whispered.

"We would have been arrested. That was so close." Papa shook his head.

We heard shouting in German. Minutes later, the patrol boat came back and passed by us. The woman and the two girls were on the deck surrounded by soldiers. Terror was written on their faces and mirrored on ours.

We caught no fish, but we had almost been caught ourselves. I shook at the thought.

Papa turned the boat around and we headed for home.

"If they had stayed in their boat, would they have drowned?" I asked.

Papa nodded.

"So maybe now they have a chance?" I asked.

"Maybe," said Papa, but he didn't sound convinced.

Three shots pierced the quiet. I trembled uncontrollably. If we had helped, there would have been two more shots.

* * *

CHAPTER 24
NEW OWNERS

MAMA LET ME STAY HOME FROM SCHOOL THE NEXT DAY. Papa did not go out in the boat. He remained in his workshop banging away. We didn't talk about what had happened the day before. It was too hard to put into words.

The following morning, I dragged myself off to school. I had missed so many classes lately. Before the invasion, I had never stayed home from school unless I had a fever. At least today, we would have art class. It was the only subject that I still enjoyed.

Our art teacher told us to draw faces of people. I drew a picture of Malka, whom I hadn't seen since her father had been taken away. My drawing really looked like her.

My mood darkened when I saw what Eric and Hans had drawn. Eric's picture had a Jew with a beard and a long nose hanging from the gallows and Hans's picture had a gang kicking a Jew on the ground. I was disgusted as my teacher complimented them on how realistically they had drawn the characters. To think that I used to be friends with Hans. I was so angry that I was about to scrunch my picture up into a ball and toss it into the garbage can. Instead, I looked at it again and put it carefully away in my school bag. I wanted to keep my picture of Malka close to me.

I had been avoiding going to see Malka since the incident with her father. I knew that we couldn't have done anything because we had been outnumbered and the soldiers had guns, but that didn't make me feel any better. I couldn't put it off any longer. I had to see if there was anything that I could do for Malka and her family.

When I stepped into the bakery, my jaw dropped. Instead of Mrs. Mendel, a cranky woman with a face like sour dough stood behind the counter.

"What are you staring at?" snapped the cranky woman.

"Excuse me, but where is Mrs. Mendel?"

The woman sneered. "She's gone."

"Gone?" All of a sudden, I felt very cold.

I didn't wait for an answer and ran upstairs and knocked. The door creaked open. I stepped in. A half-eaten dinner was still sitting on the table. Chairs were overturned. Drinks were spilt on the table, and the meat was starting to smell rotten. I ran through the apartment. It was empty. Clothes were flung all over the place, as if someone had left in the middle of packing.

I ran back downstairs to the store out of breath, not from exertion but from panic. "Where are they?" I yelled.

"You'll have to buy something first," the sour lady said smugly.

I grabbed the nearest loaf of bread and threw some coins

that Mama gave me to buy milk onto the counter. "Well?" I asked, impatiently.

"Soldiers came and arrested them. They took them away to deport them to a concentration camp."

"Was a young girl with dark ringlets, about my age, with them?"

"How should I know?"

A customer walked in. I recognized him as a regular here at the bakery. "Excuse me, sir? Do you know if the daughter of the previous owner was taken away by soldiers?" I asked. "I'm sure you've seen her helping out in the bakery."

He shook his head sadly. "Yes, my wife and I heard the commotion early this morning and looked out our window. The soldiers took her. I'm sorry. She seemed like such a sweet girl."

I muttered something and ran out of the bakery. I had to go to the train station. That was where they deported all the Jews to an unknown destination.

* * *

CHAPTER 25
TRANSIT

HUNDREDS OF JEWS WERE PACKED into the cattle trains. I felt a wave of nausea. How will I ever find her, I worried. I walked up and down blowing our secret whistle — two short, one long. Hands stretched out to me through the bars of the train, begging for help. People cried and moaned. A soldier watched me, so I kept on walking fast, still whistling. I stopped cold as I heard a return whistle. "Malka? Are you there?" I ran to a barred window. I whistled again and heard it echoed. A scared face came to the window. "Malka!" I cried.

Her hair was knotted and dirty. Her face was puffy from crying and her eyes looked so sad. Then I remembered the loaf of bread that I carried and I broke it up and squeezed the pieces through the bars and she took them.

A soldier grabbed me by the collar. "Give me your papers."

I fumbled in my pocket and pulled out my papers. The soldier studied them. "You shouldn't be here," he said.

"I just wanted to throw rocks at the dirty Jews," I lied.

"Boys will be boys." He smiled and let me go. Since he was watching me, I picked up a stone and threw it at the train, purposely missing. "Dirty Jews," I cried. This seemed to satisfy the soldier and he left me alone.

I took one last look at Malka's sad eyes as the train whistle sounded and the cars rumbled off. I stood there long after the train had disappeared. I felt empty inside.

When I got home, I turned on the radio to listen to music, but it didn't help. Every few minutes the program was interrupted by Nazi bulletins. I switched off the radio and went to my room. I took out my pencils and drew pictures of the Jews I knew who had disappeared. Then I placed a big black X over each one. I pressed so hard that the paper tore. I took out Malka's picture, but I didn't have the heart to put an X on hers. Sadly, I put her picture safely in my special box under my bed.

"Dinner," called my mother.

I joined my parents at the kitchen table. "Papa, where did all our Jewish neighbors go?"

Papa stroked his chin. "The soldiers took them away."

Like Malka. I shuddered.

"The Nazis are sending Jewish people by train to concentration camps, where they are put to work and, rumors say, they are murdered."

"I've got a headache. May I be excused?" I lied.

Mama put her hand on my forehead. "No fever, but you'd better lie down."

By the time I closed my bedroom door, I was in a panic. I had hoped my friends would get away safely before they were sent away by the Nazi soldiers. These were kids I grew up with, kids I saw every day. Now they were disappearing into thin air. No goodbyes. Just gone.

I had to check if Johan, too, had been arrested by the soldiers. It was past curfew and I knew that Mama would never allow me out. I decided to wait until my parents went to bed.

I never realized how long it took them to go to bed. Mama wanted to finish the dishes, then she ironed. Papa puttered around in his workshop, then read the paper. And when they both finally went upstairs to get ready for bed, Mama took down her hair and had to do one hundred strokes with her hairbrush. I could hear her counting. Papa took forever in the bathroom.

I lay on my bed staring at the ceiling. I was fighting hard not to fall asleep. So I took out my schoolbooks and read. I was getting far behind in school. This used to bother me, but today life bothered me more.

I had to find out what happened to Johan. Had the soldiers arrested him too or did he safely get away to Palestine? Please let him be safe, I prayed.

* * *

CHAPTER 26
PAST CURFEW

I
T WAS FINALLY QUIET IN THE HOUSE, but I read with a lantern and waited a little longer, just to make sure the coast was clear. It was eleven o'clock and I heard the sound of my father snoring. I put on dark clothes so that I could walk the streets without being noticed. Carefully, I tiptoed past their room. Mama always left the door slightly ajar, because she claimed that their room got too stuffy.

Yes, they were both fast asleep. Since I didn't want to risk the creaky stairs, I went back to my room, carefully climbed out my window, and jumped down to the ground. Brushing myself off, I kept away from the road and hid whenever a soldier walked by. It was eerie, how empty the streets were, because of the curfew. Johan's house was only a few houses away, but I had to slide along the walls of the houses to keep from being detected.

By the time I got to Johan's house, my heart was beating fast. I hesitated and then took a big breath and lifted the rock. Please let the card be there. I pried up the rock and almost cried for joy. I held the ace of spades to my heart. The soldiers didn't get you. Good luck in Palestine, my dear friend Johan. Goodbye.

Going home, I was lost in my thoughts and recklessly walked under the street lamplight.

"Halt," cried a soldier.

I froze in my tracks.

"Who goes there?" A policeman approached me. He was walking a German shepherd. The big guard dog bared his teeth and growled.

"Me, sir."

"And who is me?" he demanded.

The dog was too close for comfort. "I...I don't have my papers with me," I stammered.

"Don't you know it's past curfew?"

"Yes, sir."

"Where do you live?"

I pointed down the street.

"I'll take you home." The dog bit at my ankles and I jumped back.

"Can you pull your dog away from me?"

The policeman pulled on the leash and the dog jerked back with a yelp. "Let's go."

My legs were like rubber, but I willed them to move. We got to my house. "Thanks for walking me home, officer. Good night." I reached for the doorknob.

"Not so fast." The policeman pushed me aside and knocked on the front door.

My parents are going to kill me. I bit my lip.

My father answered the door in his nightshirt and slippers,

yawning. He sized things up pretty fast. "Hendrik, I thought you were in bed!" He looked at the policeman, then at the dog, then back at me. "Hendrik, I asked you to take my nets to my boat, but I didn't mean now. I meant first thing in the morning, silly boy."

"Sorry, Papa," I said. "I thought you meant right away," I said, playing along.

"Officer, I hope that my son didn't cause you too much of a problem."

"I'm going to have to take him to the police station for questioning."

My body stiffened like when I played frozen tag, except this wasn't a game. My life was at stake. My father looked scared and that scared me even more.

"I have something for you." Papa picked up our crystal vase that was Mama's favorite for tulips and handed it to him.

"Are you trying to bribe me?" asked the policeman in a menacing voice.

"Of course not," said Papa. "It's just a token of my appreciation for bringing my son home safely."

The policeman took the crystal vase and left. Mama would be furious.

Papa closed his eyes and took a deep breath. Then he opened them and said, "I hope you have a good explanation for all of this. You scared me out of my wits."

"What's going on?" called Mama from upstairs.

"Nothing," he called back. "Just getting myself some hot tea. I'll be up in a minute."

He whispered, "Well, I'm waiting to hear from you."

All the tension that I had been holding inside tumbled out in one sentence. "I'm sorry, Papa, but I just had to find out whether Johan and his family had been arrested or had escaped to Palestine. He promised to hide the ace of spades under a rock in his garden, if they left for Palestine." I took a deep breath and pulled it from my pocket. "Here it is! Johan and his family weren't arrested. They got out in time."

"Ah, I see," said Papa.

"Hurry up, dear" called Mama.

"Coming!" Papa ruffled my hair and I knew that everything was all right. He understood. "Good night, Hendrik," said Papa.

"Good night," I said.

"This time, go to bed and stay there."

"Yes, Papa. But what are you going to tell Mama about the vase?"

"Don't worry, I'll think of something," said Papa. To my surprise, he took one of our inexpensive drinking glasses, put it into a paper bag, and smashed it on the floor.

"What was that noise?" called Mama.

He yelled up, "I'm such a clumsy oaf. I just bumped into your favorite vase and broke it. I'll be up as soon as I clean it up."

PART THREE

RESISTANCE
1943

CHAPTER 27
FISH GUTS

IT WAS LATE BY THE TIME WE HAD CAUGHT our daily quota of fish. After we tied up our boat, I helped Papa take our catch to the Goodmans' fish market. But when we got there, a new sign was above the door and the broken window had been replaced. I was shocked to see shrimp in the window. I knew that the Goodmans would never sell shrimp because they were a forbidden food for Jewish people. I squeezed my eyes closed and there it was again — that awful memory of Mr. Mendel, being beaten in his bakery. A shudder went through my body.

I opened my eyes and peeked inside the fish market window. New owners had taken over. Barrels and baskets were everywhere. Mrs. Goodman had always kept her fish market so clean. Now there were fish guts in a pile. Mrs. Goodman never would have left that out in the open. The new owners would lose customers.

Papa saw what I saw and shook his head. I wouldn't go into the fish market with him. Papa understood and didn't force me. But he came out a few minutes later frowning. His discussion with the new owners had not gone well.

Papa would have to find another place to sell his fish. We walked around town, trying to find another fish buyer, but it was the same old story. The Jewish people had known their business and they knew how to treat their customers. The new owners, who had quickly taken over these new businesses, were inexperienced. They didn't know what they were doing. They just got a ready-made business handed to them by the government. But they didn't know how to run it.

Papa had frown lines on his forehead. We didn't talk about it. Both of us were angry. I kicked a stone on the way home. Each time I kicked it harder and further. I was hungry and mad. If I were a wasp, I would sting somebody.

When we got home, I poured out the story about the Goodmans' fish market to Mama.

Mama looked sad.

Papa threw down the newspaper. "So many Jews have disappeared. The raids are increasing. The Goodmans aren't safe."

Mama grabbed a bag and started putting things into it. "I must go over and make sure the Goodmans have enough to eat. I'll take over extra clothes. Bring me your old sweater, the one with the holes. I will mend it and give it to Pieter. We must look after our friends in any way we can."

I looked at Mama and saw her not as my mother, but as a brave woman. She tackled bad times with a stiff upper lip and did what she could to help others. I looked at Papa and he was nodding in approval. Then he smiled at her with love.

One day, I hoped that I could look at somebody with that much love and they could look back at me in the same way. I had hoped that it would be Malka. I dreamed about her at night. Sometimes it was a good dream and I saw her black ringlets bouncing and her smile that melted my heart. Other times, it was a nightmare and I saw her sad, dark eyes as she was taken away in the crowded train. I always woke up screaming at this point. I clasped my hands together and prayed. I hoped that Malka didn't mind that I did it in the Christian way, for it was the only way I knew. "I pray for your safety, Malka," I whispered. "I pray that you will come back to me and be mine."

Meanwhile, I must help Pieter and his family. I went through my things and gathered up anything that I had two of. Mama took them from me and headed out the door. I didn't mind that I was hungry and that I had to make my own supper. I was thankful that I had food to eat. Now that Pieter's father was out of a job and not allowed to work, we could give them some food and warm clothing. But how would he be able to pay rent? Would they be kicked out on the street? Where would they go? Or would they be rounded up by the Nazi soldiers first?

* * *

CHAPTER 28
ESCAPE PLAN

WHEN I GOT HOME, I TOOK OUT MY BIKE. I was feeling bitter. Things were changing too fast. I wanted things back to the way they were before the war.

Mama stopped me. "The streets aren't safe."

I was so angry that I stormed out, slamming the door. Then I trampled on her tulip garden.

Mama chased after me. "Hendrik, go to your room!"

Stamping my feet, I went back in. Where was I going anyway? The Jewish area where Pieter lived was too dangerous to visit now. There were constant raids and hoodlums looking for a fight. Besides, it was almost curfew time, so I didn't have enough time to go anywhere. I marched upstairs without taking off my muddy shoes. I knew that Mama would make me clean it up later, but right now I just felt like lashing out.

My stomach growled and the words in my book blurred. It was becoming dark outside and the house was quiet. Every time I closed my eyes, I saw poor Mr. Mendel. A stone hit my window and I jumped out of bed and ran to the window. "Pieter!"

"Help me, Hendrik."

I ran and opened the door. "Come in." Pieter looked terrible. His hair was a mess and his eyes were all puffy.

Both Mama and Papa hurried down when they heard us at the door.

"What is it?" asked Mama.

"Pieter needs our help," I said.

Mama made us hot tea. We sipped the tea and the steam tickled my nose. Pieter had always been happy and full of energy. Why were all these bad things happening to him? He didn't deserve it, just because he was Jewish.

Pieter's hands trembled. "My father has been trying to get my mother to agree to leave, ever since the Germans invaded Holland. My mother kept arguing that she couldn't leave her relatives and friends. Even when things got worse, she denied that we were in danger. She kept saying that she couldn't leave her homeland. Now it's too late."

"How do you know it's too late?" I asked.

"A messenger came to warn us. He said that he was from the underground Dutch resistance. The underground has scouts walking about town and eavesdropping on the Nazis. He told us that tomorrow night the Nazis will be rounding up the remaining Jews in Amsterdam. We will all be sent away to concentration camps."

A shiver went down my spine.

Papa cut two big slices of cheese and tore off chunks of bread. He wrapped the food in a napkin and Pieter put it into his bag.

"It's lucky that you found out ahead of time," said Papa.

"But where can we go?" asked Pieter in a small voice. "Nobody wants us."

Papa paced. "Anti-Semitism is spreading like the plague. Everybody wants a scapegoat to blame for all of our problems. Hatred is bred from ignorance and envy."

I never heard Papa speak so many words at once. Papa seemed tired out from it all and stopped pacing to sit down.

Mama cleaned a pot so much that it shined. It was her way of dealing with the situation.

Pieter looked up at my father. "Can you help me?"

Papa stroked his chin, thinking.

We waited patiently.

Papa nodded. That meant he had a plan. We all looked at him expectantly. "Do you still have a key to your fish market?"

"Yes," said Pieter. "Why?"

"You and Hendrik go immediately to the market. It will be curfew soon, so hurry. Stuff as many fish as you can carry into sacks and take them to my boat. Pieter, at dawn, bring your family to the wharf with some fishing gear. But be careful."

"Papa, what are you going to do?" I asked.

"I have to get the boat ready. Now go."

I nodded and grabbed burlap sacks and a lantern, and led Pieter out the door.

Pieter and I scooted off. It was starting to get dark and the streets were emptying fast. To avoid attracting attention, we ran from building to building, hiding whenever someone passed. We hid in the alleyway behind smelly garbage cans, waiting for the new owners to close the fish store.

We watched as they switched out the lights and locked up. They walked away briskly. Just when Pieter and I were ready to make our move, two policemen stopped right in front of the fish store, smoking cigarettes and talking. What if they stayed there all night? Pieter gave me a look of panic. I bit my nails, as we watched and waited. This was bad. It was past curfew and it was dangerous to be out in the streets.

Finally, they walked away. Pieter wanted us to move right away, but I made him wait a little longer to make sure that the coast was clear. Then we ran to the store. Pieter pulled out his key. His hand shook so much that I had to take the key from him and open the door.

"Why do I feel like a criminal breaking into our own store?" he asked.

"Because the Germans took it away from you," I said. We went inside. Pieter reached for the light switch. I knocked his hand away. "Are you crazy? People will see the light through the window."

We groped around in the dark, holding on to the wall and bumping into things. I had to risk using my lantern briefly to find the fish bin. We filled up our sacks with dead fish, working as quickly as possible. Some fell on the ground. "Leave those," I said. "We must hurry."

When we were done, Pieter took a last look around and

whispered goodbye, as we left his family's store for the very last time.

"Hurry," I said. "To the docks."

We walked, dragging the heavy sacks behind us. Attracted to the smell of fish, a scrawny stray cat, black with white spots, followed us. "Shoo," I hissed. But it kept following us. "Get lost." But it wouldn't leave. Its ribs stuck out and I felt sorry for it. The sack was so heavy that I needed to put it down for a second. "Here." I gave the stray cat a fish. It purred, licking my hand. I smiled. "Let's name him. I'm calling him Something Fishy." We picked up our sacks and kept walking. Something Fishy followed close behind.

"Halt," cried a soldier. "What are you up to?"

We stopped dead in our tracks. I didn't know what to say. I looked helplessly at Pieter.

"We were out looking for our cat," said Pieter, confidently.

Pieter's quick thinking and daring surprised me.

"So you found it. Now off with you."

We started to walk away.

"Wait," called the soldier. "What's in the sacks?"

"Fish," said Pieter.

"Open the sacks," ordered the soldier. He peeked into each sack. "Phew, that stinks. Close the sacks. Why are you carrying fish?"

"We were too late to sell our catch. So we were taking the fish home to put on ice overnight to sell them in the morning," said Pieter.

The soldier waved his hand. "Go straight home. It's past curfew."

Even though we longed to run, we walked away. Running would make us look suspicious. Pieter's lip trembled. He didn't look so brave any more.

As we neared the sea, I felt safer. The smell of the salt was reassuring and calmed my breathing down.

We reached our boat and climbed aboard. Something Fishy was still following us and I tucked him under my arm. The cat purred and licked my face. "We're safe now," I said.

"For now," whispered Pieter.

Somehow, I didn't find that reassuring.

We dumped the sacks of fish on board. "Let's go," I said.

"Where's Something Fishy?" asked Pieter.

We looked, but he was hiding somewhere on the boat. "We don't have time to look for him. We'll find him in the morning. Pieter, go home and I'll see you back here first thing in the morning for our fishing trip."

"Right," said Pieter. "Our fishing trip. And we'll be the fish that got away."

* * *

CHAPTER 29
SMUGGLING PRECIOUS CARGO

EARLY IN THE MORNING AS OTHER FISHERMEN were just arriving, the Goodmans showed up at our boat carrying fishing rods. A nervous bubble of laughter threatened to surface as I saw them all dressed like fishermen.

Papa nodded at them. Nobody said a word. Mrs. Goodman looked pale as she clutched the baby to her chest. Pieter stayed close to me.

"Hendrik, are you scared?" asked Pieter.

"Of course, I am scared. But how can I not help you?" I asked. "We're blood brothers, remember?"

Pieter hugged me. We clung to each other.

"Hurry," said Papa. "There is a trap door that leads to a little storage room where I keep supplies. I have emptied it. It is small, but you will all just fit. I will put canvas and nets on top so that the trap door is hidden. Quickly, climb in. Soldiers are patrolling the docks and harbor."

Mr. Goodman went first and reached up to help Mrs. Goodman down. Papa handed her the baby. Pieter was last to climb down. I grabbed his hand and he squeezed it, before Papa closed the trap door.

"Quickly, Hendrik, help me put the canvas tarp and nets on top of the door."

We worked fast.

"Help me throw fish on top, Hendrik. The stink should keep them from searching here." I dumped the sacks of fish over the hiding spot.

Vomiting sounds came from below. Papa's eyes and mine locked. "Stop," ordered Papa. "Move the fish away and open the trap door."

I heard a police siren getting closer. Was Papa crazy? Had he changed his mind about hiding them? But there was no time to ask questions. I pushed the fish away and opened the trap door. Papa grabbed something from his first aid kit and hurried back. We both got down on our hands and knees, and peered below. Mrs. Goodman looked green. The fish had been out all night and smelled bad. Papa gave her some ginger to chew on, knowing it helped with seasickness and nausea.

He closed the trap door and we started again, covering the door with the canvas tarp and nets, topped by a pile of dead fish from the fish store. My stomach heaved.

"Untie us, we're ready to take off," said Papa.

Normally, I felt safe on our boat. Right now, I wished to be anywhere but here. I knew too well that if we were caught helping Jews then we might be shot on the spot or sent to a concentration camp. I swallowed hard and untied the ropes. The police car pulled up to the dock, just as I pushed off and we headed out to sea.

"Stop!" a policeman cried.

My heart pounded as we kept on going.

As we made our getaway, I pretended to fish.

That was a close call. My heart beat fast, as if I were running. The winds were strong and the waves high, as they rocked our boat from side to side. Water splashed on deck, but the sea didn't scare me, not with Papa steering. Papa was a great sailor. I had seaman's legs and the tossing never bothered me because I was used to it. But I worried how the Goodmans were faring down below.

"Papa, can I let the Goodmans up for fresh air?" I asked.

"No, it's not safe," said Papa. "Keep on pretending to fish." He kept on steering further out to sea. As time passed, I felt more reassured that we could pull this off.

Suddenly, a patrol boat's siren blared. The siren got louder as it came closer. I breathed in ragged breaths. Papa took me by the shoulders. "Hendrik, the Goodmans need you. I need you. Take deep breaths. We will get through this. Grab your fishing rod and pretend to fish. Act normal." The patrol boat pulled up beside ours. Papa had no choice, but to stop the boat.

My knuckles turned white as I gripped my fishing rod. The soldiers came aboard. "Papers," demanded the officer. Papa reached into his coat and handed them over.

The officer examined them and passed them back. He glared at Papa. "Why are you so far from Holland?" he demanded.

"The fish are good here." Papa pointed to the net full of fish we brought from the fish market. I held my breath. Will the soldiers notice the fish are rotting? Will our friends be discovered? I worried.

"Search the boat," the officer commanded.

Papa scowled. His face said it all. We were in deep trouble.

They searched the boat, kicking over pails with their black boots and ripping seats apart with knives. The officer stood next to the hiding spot.

Panic rushed through me. "Sir," I said.

He spun around.

I was stalling for time. "Um..." What could I say to stop him?

The officer was growing impatient with me. "What is it you want?"

I took a deep breath and spoke. "When can I become a soldier like you?"

He smiled and mussed my hair. "When you're old enough to shave." He winked as he walked away.

The baby cried and my stomach did flip-flops as the officer turned around. He walked toward the hidden trap door.

I had to do something fast, but what? Pieter would have thought of something clever. I must not let him down.

I grabbed Something Fishy and pulled his tail making him meow.

The officer laughed. "That's some cat you have there!" He ordered his soldiers to call off the search and they climbed back into their boat. I stood watching until their boat was out of sight.

"Where did you get a cat?" asked Papa.

"He followed us last night." I stroked Something Fishy and I knew that he forgave me for pulling his tail.

"You're a fast thinker, Hendrik."

"Thank you, Papa."

* * *

CHAPTER 30
SPIRIT OF A MERMAID

THE FOG ROLLED IN. IT WAS DANGEROUS, but the mist helped hide us from the patrol boats. Now I knew that Papa would get us there safely.

I dozed off with Something Fishy purring on my chest. When I awoke, it was pitch black. Papa steered the boat without any lights. "How much longer Papa?"

"I have to go slowly, in the dark. I've arranged for a friend to meet us. I've given him the longitude and latitude. Keep your eyes open for two flashes. That's a very important job," said Papa. "It's a matter of life and death. Can you handle it?"

"Yes, Papa."

In the mist, I thought I heard a mermaid singing. I peered over the side. "Port side, a drifting cross beam from a wrecked ship."

Papa didn't question me, he jerked the boat to the right. I stared in disbelief at the long beam on the left as we passed. We had nearly hit it. If we had, it would have ruined our motor. Suddenly I saw a green flash of tail splashing in the water and, just as suddenly, it was gone.

I rubbed my eyes. Was that a mermaid warning us? Did she remember me from the time I was on Old Sea Dog's boat? Was she protecting me, too? "Thank you," I called out to the sea. I could swear that I heard a soft, sweet, melodic voice singing.

"Hendrik, it's important that you don't fall asleep. You must tell me when you see the two flashing lights. That's the signal. Remember, we're all counting on you."

"Who is your secret friend who is helping us?" I asked.

"Since our friend, Old Sea Dog is so good at smuggling and doesn't mind danger, I asked him for help. Pieter's family will be crossing on the *Mermaid*."

That would explain my visions of the mermaid. "Will Old Sea Dog take them the rest of the way to England?" I asked.

"That's too risky. He will take them to another rendezvous spot, just outside of English waters, and pass them over to an English friend of his. They will travel the last short distance by rowboat through a shallow, rocky section where neither the English nor German patrol boats can go."

I peered into the fog. Time slowly ticked on. I looked at my watch and only ten minutes had gone by. The silence and the motion of the boat made me sleepy. When my eyes started to close, I dug my nails into my fists to keep from falling asleep. I had been given an important job and I couldn't let Papa and Pieter down. I sang to keep myself awake and to calm my nerves. I had never stayed up all night before.

When I saw the light, I almost couldn't believe it was real. I was wide awake now. "Two flashes, Papa!"

Papa signalled back. He threw over the anchor. "Hurry, Hendrik, there's no time to lose." We quickly shovelled away the stinking, rotting fish and, together, Papa and I lifted off the nets and canvas, exposing the trap door. Papa grabbed hold of the iron ring and opened the door. He stuck his head into the hole and said, "Time to switch boats."

Pieter crawled out gasping for air. Fish slid from Mr. Goodman's head. Mrs. Goodman held out the baby to Papa as she staggered out.

"Pieter, will we see each other again?" I asked, all choked up.

"I'm sure we will." Pieter hugged me tight.

Our fingers touched. "Friends, forever," we whispered together.

Old Sea Dog brought the *Mermaid* alongside our boat. He threw a rope and I tied it up to our boat and helped him aboard. "I saw the mermaid," I told him.

"Ah, then this will be a safe trip for all involved," he said.

Relief flooded over me. I now believed that my best friend and his family would make it safely across to freedom.

They soon boarded the *Mermaid* together. The boat disappeared into the fog. My best friend was gone and headed for freedom.

We headed back home. "It's over," I sighed.

Papa looked me in the eye. "For you it's over, but for me it's only the beginning."

"What do you mean?"

"There are many people to save. I need to keep helping. I must do whatever I can."

"Me, too, Papa."

* * *

CHAPTER 31
FREE NETHERLANDS

PAPA AND I WENT OUT IN THE BOAT. We were smuggling a Jewish family, the Cohens, to freedom, just like we had done for Pieter's family. Today the German patrol boats were everywhere and I feared that our luck would run out.

Mrs. Cohen had been in Mama's knitting circle for years. Mama and she were very good friends. I felt very good about what I was doing. My stomach was nervous, but that was the price that I had to pay.

Mrs. Cohen and her family had been hiding in the attic of a farmer's barn, before it became too dangerous. The soldiers had been ransacking houses, looking for trap doors, ripping apart rooms, leaving nothing in one piece. Spies for the Nazis were everywhere. No one could be trusted.

Mrs. Cohen knew that it was just a matter of time until their hiding place would be discovered. She risked leaving the barn to visit my mother pleading to her for help. My mother didn't hesitate and brought us into the scheme to save their lives.

We headed out to the North Sea. It was a difficult trip because we were stopped three times. Three times Papa and I had to make up stories about how our engine kept stalling and how the strong currents pulled us out way past the boundaries. Three times we had to pretend to head back toward Holland and then, when the patrol boat was gone, change direction and swing back toward England. Fortunately, it was a different patrol boat each time.

We finally met up with Old Sea Dog. Old Sea Dog was like a pirate. He knew how to sail in dangerous rocky waters where the patrol boats dared not go. He then met his trusted English friend, known to us as the "Captain," who rowed the fugitives to safely.

When we returned from our special 'fishing' trip, Papa went to sell the fish we had caught while I headed for home. I heard footsteps on the pavement behind me. I glanced over my shoulder and saw a boy following me. Adrenaline shot through me. I couldn't trust anybody. I turned around and faced him, ready for a fight. "What do you want?"

"Have you heard of the underground organization called the 'Free Netherlands'?" he asked.

I was wary. "What's it to me?" I asked.

"Do you know the Cohens?" he asked.

"No," I lied.

"I know that you and your father smuggled them out."

"Who told you that?" I asked.

"We have ears and eyes everywhere."

I tensed up. "Are you going to arrest us?"

"No, we're on the same side. We are the underground

Dutch resistance. We forge passports and courier secret documents outside the Netherlands. We help Jews hide and escape. We need your help, too."

"Why didn't you ask my father?"

"Two kids talking are less suspicious than two adults. Spies are everywhere."

I sighed. "What do you want?" I asked.

"We want you and your father to stow away families in your boat and take them to specific destinations. We can pay you."

"If you have heard of my father and me, then you will know that we don't take money," I said.

The boy nodded. "I didn't mean to show disrespect."

"No harm done," I said.

"Can we count on your help?" he asked.

"I don't know."

"I have contacts in different countries and in the concentration camps. Give me a list of your friends and I can find out what happened to them."

"Malka Mendel." I felt a lump in my throat.

"I will find her for you. You have my word."

That made up my mind for me. "Yes, I will help," I said. We shook on it.

Suddenly, the air raid went off. "I must hurry to the shelter. When will I see you again?"

"You won't, but I will send a messenger. She will arrange the meeting. She will be known to you only as 'Pigeon.'"

Like the carrier pigeons carrying secret messages, I thought.

"In case you are caught and tortured, we don't want you to blurt out any real names," he explained.

I gulped. I could be arrested and tortured. This was not a game.

"My code name is Lightning. If I don't live, I will make sure that someone in the resistance finds your friend, Malka Mendel for you."

I was going to say more, but the boy disappeared into the dark night.

* * *

CHAPTER 32

SORROW

A S I HEADED HOME, I saw a plane flying low in the sky. Suddenly, Nazi aircraft guns started shooting at it. As the air raid sounded, I changed direction and hurried to the nearest underground shelter.

I pounded on the door with my fist. "Open up, let me in."

The door swung open and I joined a dozen Dutch people cramped up in small, dark room below the building. We waited anxiously as the sounds of bombs and gunfire filled the air. As I looked around at my neighbors, I could see that everyone in Holland was suffering from this war. The smell of fear filled the room. One person rocked back and forth, another bit his fingernails, while others clung to each other for comfort. Finally, the all-clear siren wailed and we left the cramped space to head for home.

Papa hadn't returned home from the fish market after the air raid. Mama was beside herself with worry. I combed the streets looking for him. I didn't care if the night was dangerous. I needed to find my father. I searched streets, alleys, bars, restaurants. As time ticked by, I felt more and more frantic. I ran home hoping that he had shown up.

"Has Papa come home yet?" I asked.

Mama's eyes were red from crying. "Not yet. Just keep looking. He needs us."

I rushed out and retraced my steps, just in case I had missed him. And then I saw something that made me stop in my tracks. I saw his old blue cap that Mama had knitted for him. "Papa," I cried. I ran closer to a pile of bricks and debris and started digging with my hands like a dog.

I threw off the bricks to free him. I could tell he wasn't breathing. I held him to my chest crying, "Papa! Papa!" as tears streamed down my face.

I wailed like a wolf at the moon. Papa had not made it safely to the shelter. A bomb had exploded beside him. A stranger came by. "Let me help you carry him to the hospital." I looked up at the man standing there patiently, waiting for me. Deep down, I knew that it was too late.

When we got to the hospital, they put Papa on a stretcher. A doctor examined Papa and covered his body with a sheet. "I'm sorry," he said. "I wish that I could spend more time with you, but there are so many others waiting." He looked very tired. "You can use that phone over there." He pointed and then left.

"What's your phone number? I'll ring your family for you," said the kind man who helped me. I noticed for the first time that the man was covered in blood.

"I'd better make that call myself," I said.

It was the hardest thing I had ever done. "Mama," I choked, "It's Papa."

"Is he hurt?" she interrupted.

"He's..." There was no gentle way to say this.

"He's what?" asked Mama anxiously.

"He's dead." I broke down and cried.

Mama screamed, "Noooooo!"

I didn't know how long I held the phone, both of us sobbing. I somehow managed to give her the name of the hospital and waited for her to arrive. A nurse saw the blood all over me. "Are you hurt?" she asked.

I shook my head no, but I was hurting so badly inside.

* * *

CHAPTER 33
THE PASSWORD

AS MAMA STOOD BESIDE ME AT THE FUNERAL, she looked so frail. "I promise I'll take care of you, Mama." I draped my arm around her. Some of her friends led her away. I stayed a little longer to say goodbye to Papa. I was lost in my own thoughts.

A pretty young girl with high cheekbones tapped me on my shoulder. She wore a kerchief, but her two blond braids stuck out the sides. Her torn coat was patched and her shoes scuffed. "I'm sorry for your loss."

"Who are you?"

"Pigeon," she answered.

"Pigeon?" I repeated. Then I remembered the password and my promise to help. But I was enraged and I turned on her. "How dare you bother me at a time like this?"

"I'm sorry for your loss, but other lives are at stake and we cannot wait." She fingered the cross around her neck.

I glared at her. She didn't look more than fifteen, my age. She was tiny, but she stood so tall with her shoulders back. When I started to walk, she blocked my way. "You have a lot of nerve," I said as I tried to move past her.

Once again she moved to stop me.

"Can't take no for an answer?" I hissed, angrily.

"No, I can't and I won't." She stared me down with her blue eyes.

I liked the fire in her eyes and her spirit. "Okay, convince me." My arms were crossed.

"We need you," she replied simply.

"Time's up. Goodbye." This time I got past her.

"Wait," she called.

I kept on walking.

She shouted after me, "Your father would have wanted you to keep helping people."

I turned around to face her. "What do you want of me?"

"To smuggle out Jews in your fishing boat."

"Who are you?" I demanded.

"Welcome to the Free Netherlands and its underground resistance. The pay is nothing and the hours are midnight until dusk. If you are caught, the benefits are few. At worst, you will get shot. At best, you will be sent to a concentration camp and gassed to death. Do you accept the job or not?"

"Why are you risking death? You're not even Jewish," I challenged.

"I am human and that's what people should do, help each other. I really care about the Jewish families and their misfortune. Their family and friends are being killed and they have no place to turn. They can't count on anyone. And I hate the Nazis. I couldn't live with myself during these horrible times, if it weren't for my work with the underground. Are you with me or not?"

"I'm with you."

She smiled. "Good. You begin at midnight."

"Tonight?"

"You heard me. I will deliver two Jewish children at the stroke of midnight to your boat. Hide them. Your friend, Old Sea Dog, is part of the Free Netherlands and has already been notified. He has agreed to meet you and take the children at the pre-arranged meeting spot." She took out a piece of paper and handed it to me. "Here are the coordinates."

I looked at the piece of paper. On it were written the longitude and latitude of the meeting place.

"Memorize it and tear it up," said Pigeon.

I looked at it again and then I tore it up into many pieces. 'Thank you, Papa for teaching me how to read longitude and latitude,' I said in my head.

"Good luck." She stuck out her hand.

I don't know what came over me. I figured if I were going to die, I wanted to die happy. I leaned over and quickly kissed her. Her eyes flew open and my face flushed. I didn't know which of us was more surprised.

* * *

CHAPTER 34

WORKING FOR THE UNDERGROUND

RIGHT ON TIME, PIGEON DELIVERED the scrawny children to my boat. Without wasting time, I hid them below the deck. I went to say goodbye to Pigeon, but she had already disappeared into the night. Without any lights, I steered out of the docks. I didn't relax until I was out at sea. I navigated by using the stars, the way Papa had taught me. The North Star shone bright in the night sky showing the way. I kept a lookout for patrol boats.

Sure enough, I heard the siren. Was this finally it? Was my life over? My heart pounded as the patrol boat neared mine. I messed up my hair and tried to look half asleep.

A Nazi boarded my boat. He waved his gun at me. "Papers!"

My identity documents were always on me. I faked a big yawn and stretched. Then I reached into my pockets and handed him my papers.

"They seem in order. But what is a fishing boat doing out in the middle of the night?" he demanded. He pointed his gun at me.

I yawned again. "Sorry, I fell asleep at the wheel. My parents will be sick with worry. I'm in for a big thrashing."

"Yeah, I fell asleep at work once and I was fined. I know how it is. Are you going to head back now?" he asked.

I scratched my head. "It's dangerous to travel at night and I have to be out here at daybreak. So it makes more sense to just anchor here and wait until daylight." I held my breath, praying that the Nazi would buy my tale.

"You might as well," agreed the soldier and left.

The blood was pounding in my ears. I had feared that these were my last moments. I tried to drink a cup of coffee from my thermos, but my hands were shaking so badly that I spilled it. It took a long time for me to calm down. I checked on the two hidden children. Asleep, they looked like angels.

The current was with me and I was early for the meeting spot with Old Sea Dog, so I anchored. The rocking of the boat lulled me to sleep.

* * *

CHAPTER 35

DOLPHIN

IN MY HALF-SLUMBER, I REMEMBERED A TIME when Papa and I were fishing...

Everything was good, here in the boat. We didn't say a word as the boat rocked back and forth and we caught lots of fish.

Papa had his nets out and was busy hauling one up when I heard squealing and ran to look.

"Papa! A dolphin is caught in our net."

"So it is," said Papa.

"We have to let it go." Papa didn't move to free it.

"They do eat a lot of fish. You could say they compete with us."

The dolphin looked up at me with its big pleading eyes. "It's so beautiful. We have to let it go," I repeated.

"I've heard that dolphins are good luck," said Papa. "Many stories have been told of how ships have gone down in storms and dolphins have saved the fisherman, carrying them to shore. What do you think, Hendrik? Do you think that these tales are true?" Papa's eyes were smiling.

"Yes, Papa. I do believe in the dolphins. They are good luck." I heard another squeal coming from the sea. The boat was surrounded by a group of other dolphins. They were all

squealing back and forth to our caught dolphin, who answered in a forlorn cry.

Carefully, Papa lowered the net into the water, tilting it and losing some of our catch for the day. With the net tilted, the dolphin was able to free itself and it swam out to freedom. The other dolphins gathered round it, bumping noses and squealing with delight. Our dolphin squeaked happily and flipped in the air. Splashed by the water, I laughed and waved goodbye as the dolphins swam off into the distance.

"Well, Hendrik, you got your wish, but now we will have to stay late to catch more fish."

"That's okay, Papa. I don't mind." And I didn't. I knew that freedom was the most valuable thing of all.

A foghorn sounded and I jumped. Now I was wide awake and reality hit me like an ice-cold bucket of water. Old Sea Dog's boat, the *Mermaid* pulled beside the *Freedom*. I carried the two children up to the deck. I woke them and they boarded the *Mermaid*, waving goodbye to me. I waved back and watched until they were out of sight.

* * *

EPILOGUE
RIGHTEOUS AMONG THE NATIONS
2000

JET-LAGGED FROM TRAVELING between Holland and Israel, I find myself here at Yad Vashem, a complex located on the Mount of Remembrance in Jerusalem. It is a vast, sprawling site of tree-studded walkways leading to museums, exhibits, archives, monuments, sculptures, and memorials, all dedicated to documenting the history of the Jewish people during the Holocaust. This is also a sacred space to which almost two million visitors come annually. I have been invited to Yad Vashem to be honored for my deeds during World War II.

As I wander on my own, I pass many exhibits that are heart wrenching, especially the Children's Memorial, an underground cavern. The flames of memorial candles flicker in the darkness like tiny stars representing the 1.5 million Jewish children who perished in the Holocaust.

I head over to the Garden of the Righteous Among Nations. That's where today's ceremony will be held. I spend a lot of time walking among the lines of trees planted in honor of non-Jewish men and women who risked their lives in order to save Jews. I read the marble plaques engraved with names of the rescuers arranged according to country. Today, both Papa's and my name will be added. Papa would be so proud if he were here with me now.

I remember the day not so long ago when a stranger came to my house in Amsterdam. He told me that he was from Israel and represented the Holocaust Martyrs' and Heroes Remembrance Authority, the official Israeli institution for preserving the memory of the Holocaust.

I recall telling him that I had never heard of this group.

He went on to explain that Yad Vashem keeps the memory of the six million Jewish victims of the Holocaust alive. It also honors the non-Jews who risked their lives to save Jews during the Nazi period.

"But why are you here?" I had asked him.

"You and your late father are to be honored in Israel," he told me, "for your heroic and humanitarian actions in helping Jews during World War II."

"But how did you find out about what we did?" I asked, with surprise.

"Many Jewish survivors whom you saved gave your names," he answered.

I was overwhelmed with emotion, but began to plan for our trip to Israel.

My thoughts are jolted back to the present as a man bumps into me. I turn to find Katarina, my wife.

"Hendrik, there are so many people gathered here to honor you." She squeezes my hand and I kiss her affectionately on the cheek. "It's hard to believe that fifty-five years have passed since the war."

"And you are just as beautiful as the day I met you," I say. "Can you believe that we were both only fifteen at the time? My beautiful Pigeon." I still like to call her by her password, my pet name for her. "You, too, were courageous."

My mind strays to Malka, my first love, whom I have never forgotten. I still have the picture that I drew of her. In my memory she remains a young girl forever.

After the war, I got a phone call from a stranger. He said that his name was Lightning. I felt a shock run through me. "I found out what happened to your friend."

He had been true to his word. "Malka Mendel. Is she alive?" I had asked.

"No, I am so sorry." He went on to tell me her fate. It turned out that the cattle train, where I had seen her, took her to Westerbork, the concentration camp in Holland. From there, she and her family were sent to Auschwitz, the death camp.

I wipe a tear from my cheek.

Jacob also will not be here. After the war, I found out that before Jacob and his family could get their false passports to escape, they were arrested. Later the Nazis shot them in cold blood.

I never talk much about the war. Today I am a quiet man, retired with two wonderful sons and four grandchildren. I still live in Holland and I still love to fish in my boat. My eldest son surprised us and named his daughter Malka to honor my dear friend. Katarina and I were both deeply moved. My granddaughter is the same age as Malka was when she was taken away. It's my granddaughter who likes to go fishing with me. We mostly talk without words — just like Papa and I used to do.

"Look who's here," says Katarina, interrupting my thoughts.

I embrace Johan, who lives in Israel with his wife, four children, and ten grandchildren. We hug and talk until an official goes to the microphone and announces, "Everyone, please take your seats."

I look at the crowd. "Why are there so many people here?"

"The Jewish people you saved now have children and grandchildren of their own. All of these families were touched by you," explains Johan.

Katarina smiles and says, "Isn't this exciting? These people have come from Israel, Europe, the United States, and Canada to tell their personal stories and give thanks to you and your father."

"Oh, my goodness, there's Pieter! All the way from Canada." I wave madly to Pieter in the crowd. He sees me and waves back. I knew that he would be here. My best friend, forever.

"Do you have your speech ready?" Katarina asks.

I take out the notes from my pocket and look them over. My written speech explains that my father was a good example to follow. He was a righteous person who would have helped anyone. After his death, I found the inner strength to carry on his legacy, hiding and transporting Jewish families to freedom.

But when I am called up to give my speech, I throw away my notes and the years slip away as I start at the beginning. "Everything changed for me the day I turned twelve. My father taught me never to wait for someone else to help, because it is up to each of us to take personal action. I remember as if it were yesterday. We got an SOS call on our radio. My father insisted on rescuing a French couple who were stranded at sea and I wanted to go home to celebrate my twelfth birthday..."

* * *

courtesy Yad Vashem

The Garden of the Righteous Among the Nations, located at Yad Vashem, the Holocaust Museum in Israel. "Righteous Among the Nations" or "Righteous Gentile" is the name given to non-Jews who aided and saved Jews during the Holocaust. A tree is planted for each of these people; each one may have saved one Jew, maybe a thousand or more. A Hebrew saying states that "if you save one person it is as if you have saved the world."

An original German cattle-car, given to Yad Vashem by
Polish authorities, rests on a train track. This car was used to
transport Jews to concentration camps in Europe.

הם ידעו כמים של שקט וכי

וימי שפל שבהם נאלצו ליטול את מקל הנדודים,
לחפש מקומות חדשים ולשקם את קהילותיהם.
בכל מקום בו ישבו תרמו מכישרונם לעמים שבקרבם חיו.

בבקעה זו יישמר זכרם לעד.

THIS MEMORIAL COMMEMORATES THE JEWISH COMMUNITIES DESTROYED
BY NAZI GERMANY AND ITS COLLABORATORS. AND THE FEW WHICH SUFFERED
BUT SURVIVED IN THE SHADOW OF THE HOLOCAUST.

FOR MORE THAN A THOUSAND YEARS JEWS LIVED IN EUROPE. ORGANIZING
COMMUNITIES TO PRESERVE THEIR DISTINCT IDENTITY.
IN PERIODS OF RELATIVE TRANQUILITY JEWISH CULTURE FLOURISHED.
BUT IN PERIODS OF UNREST JEWS WERE FORCED TO FLEE.
WHEREVER THEY SETTLED. THEY ENDOWED
THE PEOPLE AMONGST WHOM THEY LIVED WITH THEIR TALENTS.

HERE THEIR STORIES WILL BE TOLD.

The Valley of the Communities at Yad Vashem names over
5,000 Jewish communities that were destroyed or barely
survived the Holocaust. The stone reads: *This memorial
commemorates the Jewish communities destroyed by Nazi
Germany and its collaborators, and the few which suffered but
survived in the shadow of the Holocaust.*

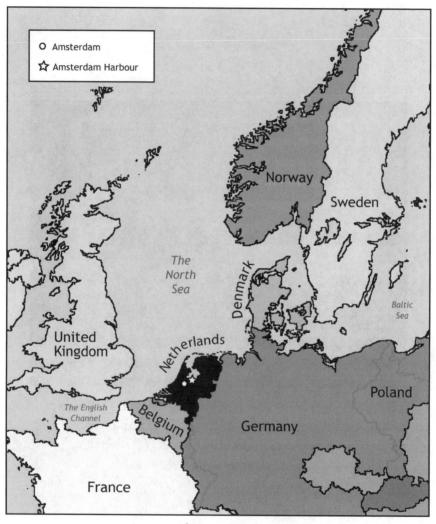

A map of Europe in 1940.

A man stands beneath a sign indicating the entrance to the
Jewish quarter of Amsterdam, where Hendrik's Jewish friends
lived.

USHMM, courtesy of Francisca Verdoner Kan

Schoolchildren pose for a class photo during in Amsterdam during the war. The Jewish children can been seen wearing the Star of David.

USHMM, courtesy of Harry Goldsmith

A close up of a Dutch Jewish star with the word Jood (Dutch for Jew) printed on it. It was mandatory for Jews to wear this star at all times.

Dutch Jews being deported to the Westerbork concentration camp. Hendrik's friends were sent to Westerbork, as it was used as a transit camp for Dutch Jews before they were sent to Auschwitz and other death camps for extermination. Anne Frank was one of the 100,000 people who were sent to this camp.

Jewish refugees, much like the ones that Hendrik helped, are ferried out of Denmark aboard a Danish fishing boat.

German soldiers patrol a harbour in Amsterdam to prevent the unauthorized use of Danish boats for smuggling goods and people. There were strict penalties such as deportation to a concentration camp for anyone caught smuggling.

A poster advertising the anti-Semitic propaganda film *De ewige Jude* (The Eternal Jew) hangs on the side of a Dutch building. This poster is an example of the propaganda the Nazis used to influence people like Hendrik's teacher and classmates.

A Dutch policeman crouches inside a small bunker that served as a hiding place for Dutch Jews during the war. Entire families would hide in spaces as small as these, in hopes of remaining undiscovered by the Nazis.

A Danish fishing boat like the one owned by Hendrik's father is on display at the US Holocaust Memorial Museum.